D0361529

Abelard's Love

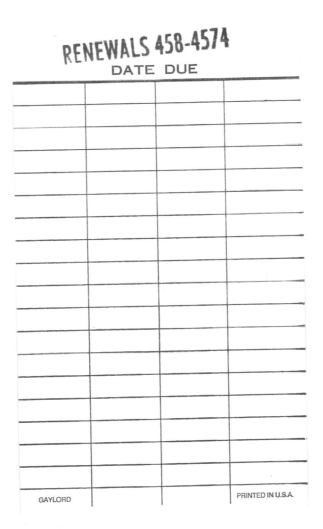

RENEWALS 458-4574

DATE DUE

GAYLORD

PRINTED IN U.S.A.

European Women
Writers Series

EDITORIAL BOARD

Marion Faber
Swarthmore College
Alice Jardine
Harvard University
Susan Kirkpatrick
University of California,
San Diego
Olga Ragusa
Columbia University

Abelard's Love

ABAELARDS LIEBE

LUISE RINSER

Translated by Jean M. Snook

University of Nebraska Press
Lincoln and London

Library
University of [illegible]
of San [illegible]

© S. Fischer Verlag GmbH,
Frankfurt am Main, 1991
Introduction and translation
© 1998 by the University of
Nebraska Press. Published by
arrangement with S. Fischer
Verlag GmbH, Frankfurt am Main.
All rights reserved. Manufactured
in the United States of America.
♾ The paper in this book
meets the minimum requirements
of American National Standard for
Information Sciences – Permanence
of Paper for Printed Library
Materials, ANSI Z39.48-1984.
Library of Congress Cataloging-in-
Publication Data.
Rinser, Luise, 1911– [Abaelards
Liebe. English] Abelard's love = [Abaelards
Liebe] / Luise Rinser: translated by
Jean M. Snook.   p.   cm. –
(European women writers series)
ISBN 0-8032-3914-9 (cloth : alk. paper)
ISBN 0-8032-8968-5 (pbk. : alk. paper)
1. Abelard, Peter, 1079–1142 –
Fiction. 2. Héloïse, 1101–1164 –
Fiction. I. Snook, Jean M., 1952–   .
II. Title.   III. Series.
PT2635.I68A6198   1998
833'.912–dc21   97–14767 CIP

Library
University of Texas
at San Antonio

❀❀❀❀❀❀❀❀❀❀❀❀❀❀❀❀❀❀❀❀❀
❀   ❀

CONTENTS

WITHDRAWN
UTSA LIBRARIES

WITHDRAWN
UTSA LIBRARIES

TRANSLATOR'S INTRODUCTION

Luise Rinser's life spans the twentieth century. She was born 30 April 1911 in the small south German town of Pitzling in Upper Bavaria and grew up immersed in the rich Roman Catholic culture of the region. Its magnificent baroque churches and the symbolism and pageantry of the liturgy hold continuing appeal for her. Rinser has strong early memories of summer holidays spent at the Benedictine convent in Wessobrunn, where the nuns still sing Gregorian chant. It was there that the earliest German poetess, Diemut, lived around 1100. It is there that Rinser has arranged to be buried.

Luise was the only child of Josef Rinser, a school principal and church organist, and his wife Luise, née Sailer. She had a privileged childhood, took violin lessons, and made frequent trips to Munich to attend concerts. This early immersion in music is evident in her smooth, flowing prose. And her understanding of music and musicians has brought her together with some of the most significant people in her life: her first husband, the pianist and conductor Hans-Günther Schnell; her second husband, the composer Carl Orff; and her friend, the Korean-German composer Isang Yun. As she explains in her reader *Fliessendes Licht* (1993; Flowing light), Yun's orchestral pieces *Dimensions* and *Distances* represent acoustically the three levels that, in medieval European mystery plays, represent the whole scheme of creation: most of us live on the lowest level of conflict and war, the middle level is occupied by those with the wisdom and vision to lead us out of our distress, and the upper level contains the highest power, eternal harmony and peace. It is Rinser's conviction that this highest power does exist that guides her, enables her to hope, and inspires her interest in historical and contemporary accounts of exceptional individuals who devote their lives to bettering the situation of others.

Peter Abelard was one such man with vision. He pointed the way from rote recital of the creed to the substantiation of one's belief through dialectic reasoning. His emphasis on critical thought was a message of definite appeal to Rinser. Her own insistence on reason has won her the friendship and support of others similarly inclined to question common assumptions. This same trait has also brought her into conflict with and cost her heavy losses at the hands of more doctrinaire thinkers.

Rinser has always been more interested in the individual than the group. She studied psychology and pedagogy and was attracted to the innovative teaching methods of Pestalozzi, the Swiss educational reformer who encouraged self-expression rather than rote learning. When she graduated from the University of Munich in 1934, the Nazis had already come to power. She refused to join the party and was therefore unable to get a teaching job in a major center. Instead she was given a post as the only teacher in an isolated community of impoverished peat cutters. By 1939, it was mandatory for all teachers to be members of the National Socialist Party. Rinser adroitly avoided getting fired by resigning her post to marry Hans-Günther Schnell a little earlier than they had planned.

With Schnell she had two sons, Christoph and Stephan, and while home with them began to write in earnest. Her first book-length story, *Die gläsernen Ringe* (1941; The glassy rings), is a semiautobiographical account of a young girl growing up in Wessobrunn; it ends with her commitment to a life guided not by "the confused, dark suffering of minions, but by the sharp, clear law of the spirit." This bold statement in repressive times brought her a congratulatory letter from the German novelist Hermann Hesse (who was living in Switzerland), and a prompt publication ban from the Nazis. Her courageous publisher, Peter Suhrkamp, continued to encourage her writing and send her financial support until he himself was arrested. Hans-Günther

Schnell was killed in action in 1943, and Luise was denounced and arrested for high treason in 1944. Her "treason" consisted of stating the obvious to a worried friend who feared that her husband too might be killed in action. Rinser said the war would not last much longer, since the Germans were clearly losing, and that the woman's husband should be primarily concerned with keeping himself alive until hostilities ceased. For that, Rinser was incarcerated in the infamous Traunstein prison, where she endured starvation, intense cold, and untreated infections and did hard labor while awaiting a trial that never took place. Only the end of the war saved her from even worse conditions in a concentration camp. Rinser did manage to keep a prison journal until she ran out of paper. It was published in 1946, under the title *Gefängnis-Tagebuch* (Prison diary). With typical tenacity, Rinser subsequently worked for prison reform, spoke on women's rights, and cofounded the Lessing Society for the Promotion of Tolerance.

Rinser has always asked questions, and the question mark has become a characteristic feature of her style that is traceable from her earliest correspondence. In *Abelard's Love* Astrolabe, the son of Abelard and Heloise, asks personal questions that advance the plot, and Abelard's theological questions are landmarks in the intellectual history of the Catholic Church. As one might expect, Rinser's friends within the Church have been mainly Jesuits, highly educated thinkers and reformers who are ultimately answerable only to the Pope. One she identifies only as M., the other was the celebrated theologian Karl Rahner. Rinser herself was one of the journalists authorized to follow the proceedings of Vatican II.

Rinser is extremely well read and informed about world events. She likes to spend the first four hours of the day reading, and she watches the evening news on television. In the winter she makes her home in Rocca di Papa near Rome. In the summer she goes north to her apartment in Munich. Over the years she has traveled widely. She was in Cape Canaveral as a journalist when the Americans sent their first manned rocket into space. Since then she has given lectures throughout the United States and been well received in North and South Korea. In 1984 she was the Green Party's candidate for the position of federal president of Germany.

Since 1970 Rinser has published consecutive chronicles containing extensive critical commentary on current issues. These are more in the nature of journals than diaries and as such form a valuable contribution to the documentation of the twentieth century.

It is the novels and short stories, though, on which Rinser's fame is based. These are structurally and thematically diverse. The short stories date from 1937 and have as their protagonists children, young people, housewives, businessmen, social outcasts, and the dying. Their settings range through Germany's prewar years and war years, its postwar poverty, then prosperity, industrial success, and the ensuing ecological activism.

Rinser has never shied away from difficult material: the labyrinthine passages of the mind or the grim realities of wartime. Regardless of the subject matter, her style remains economical and flowing, the result of her own ruthless editing. Her aim is to write lucidly for a broad audience, to communicate with the general reader as well as with intellectuals. Over the years she has acquired a large readership and receives on average five letters a day from readers throughout the world in response to her works. She is intensely interested in other people, answers all correspondence, and welcomes countless visitors to her home. To Rinser, this interaction is more important than critics' reviews.

If there is a common contributing cause for the success of Rinser's books, it is her infectious interest in the characters she creates. The plot always centers around a small number of characters who are empathetically portrayed in all their complexity. While they may be critical of each other, Rinser shows each one as an individual affected by a unique set of circumstances. The narrative point of view is most often that of one of the characters. *Abelard's Love* is narrated by Astrolabe, but his continuing engagement with and reactions to the other characters allows them a kind of character development. Rinser's characters are not stereotypical representations of good or evil. They are sometimes right, sometimes wrong. They make mistakes, miss chances, and are handicapped by aspects of their own personalities. Rinser feels that most criminals need a psychiatrist, not a judge. Although gratuitous violence and racism are present in her works, the perpetrators are peripheral figures. Rinser is more interested in pointing the way toward good than in focusing, even for condemnatory purposes, on outright evil. Anyone she takes the trouble to portray from within is a sympathetic character. Rinser respects human life and lets her characters explain themselves at length.

Abelard's Love is Rinser's thirteenth novel and perhaps her last, the product of over fifty years' experience and growth as a writer. It is her third novel based on figures from religious history. In 1975 she wrote a novel for young people, *Bruder Feuer* (Brother Fire), a popularization of the life of St. Francis of Assisi (1181–1226), founder of the Franciscan order. Her next novel, *Mirjam* (1983; Miriam), is a direct interior monologue written from the point of view of Mary Magdalene after the Crucifixion. This powerful novel ranks among Rinser's best and is structurally the precursor of *Abelard's Love*.

Both *Miriam* and *Abelard's Love* are sustained reflections on the lives of important figures by people associated with but tangential to them. Both Miriam and Astrolabe are deeply affected by past events. Both works also contain a central image, something new in Rinser's writing style. The central image in *Abelard's Love* is the image of light. Asked by his professor, Abelard, what he thinks about the Trinity and the Holy Ghost, Astrolabe answers by saying that he has an image of three candles. Held together, they make one flame; held apart, each has its own flame. The one flame is simultaneously in all three.

With the image of the three candles, Rinser links Abelard's controversial teachings about the Trinity with his equally controversial personal life. The Trinity consists of the Father, the Son, and the Holy Ghost. Abelard is a father, Astrolabe is his son, and the wife and mother, Heloise, heads the convent of the Holy Ghost, or Paraclete.

Rather than using the flame, or fire, image simply as a unifying leitmotif with limited meaning, Rinser expands her application of it to include the passion and purification it connotes and the destruction it denotes. It is the flame of passion between Abelard and Heloise, the purifying force of love, but it is also the fire set by the Church to burn Abelard's condemned work on the Trinity and to burn "heretics" at the stake.

[xi]

A secondary image that runs through *Abelard's Love* also undergoes an interesting transformation. It is the image of Jephthah's daughter, who apparently offered no resistance to being sacrificed. Astrolabe initially equates her with Heloise, seeing Abelard as the father who sacrificed her by sending her to the convent. By analogy, Astrolabe also thinks of the story of Abraham and Isaac, of another father who was willing to sacrifice his child. Jephthah's daughter was sacrificed. Isaac was not, because God intervened at the last moment. Using logic not devoid of humor, Astrolabe then compares himself to both Jephthah's daughter and Isaac, with the difference that he feels he has been bound to the altar and neither sacrificed nor saved but simply left there, year after year, abandoned by his parents and so inhibited that he is fit only to become a canon, a clergyman serving in a cathedral.

Astrolabe is torn between two worlds and not entirely at home in either. Raised by his paternal aunt, Denise, in Brittany, he loves the countryside and rural life, yet he has been well educated by a private tutor and feels drawn to study in Paris. Once there, he realizes that his capabilities are only average, and he is repulsed by the intrigues and squalor of the big city. On a visit home, he is tempted to stay. He rolls in the grass for joy and from that vantage point finds the philosophical debates of the academics absolutely ludicrous: "What came first: the grass or the idea of grass? Ridiculous problems, artificial, crazy." The undeniable fact, though, is that he is not a simple farm boy but the natural son of two of the greatest thinkers of the day, Abelard and Heloise. For that reason Denise dissuades him from staying in the country, and Heloise procures him a safe position in keeping with his modest abilities, that of a canon. Astrolabe feels, with justification, that he has been shelved.

The critic Harry Zohn accurately describes the novel as "an anguished 'J'accuse' of epic dimensions . . . a sort of psychoanalysis à trois" that "carries a considerable cargo of thought and emotion." Astrolabe's problem is not the overbearing parent, but the absent parent. He speaks for all who want and would benefit from more nurturing and guidance. His lonely struggle for identity poignantly illustrates the conundrum of the moderately gifted, whose joy is sullied by feelings of inadequacy. Abelard is the exception; Astrolabe is the rule.

With Astrolabe as her main character, Rinser evaluates Abelard through the eyes of a pragmatist, showing the personal consequences of his consuming professional pursuits. Abelard does not emerge as a hero or saint in the novel. In 1970, Rinser published *Unterentwickeltes Land Frau* (Underdeveloped country woman), a meticulously researched and severe criticism of the church through the ages, primarily of its suppression of women. (Sales of the book run in the hundreds of thousands.) Having worked her way through to this position, Rinser obviously could not wholeheartedly endorse a man who forced his young wife to enter a convent, regardless of his revolutionary contribution to European thought in the early Middle Ages. One senses that Luise Rinser's sympathies lie with her namesake, whose letters to Abelard have taken their place in world literature.

Rinser's individuals are both real and representative. *Abelard's Love* is replete with comparative references, a technique Rinser employs to add depth and to forestall her characters' being judged in isolation. Abelard's choice of monastic life for himself and Heloise seems less unkind in light of the fact that his parents voluntarily made the same decision for themselves. The envious reaction of Heloise's guardian, Fulbert, to her relationship with Abelard has a model in Roman mythology, in Hephaestus's envy of the lovers Mars and Venus, and the course of Abelard's professional and personal life shows surprising parallels to the life of St. Augustine, who lived seven hundred years earlier. Such examples, by their presence, plead for greater understanding of the main characters' fates.

Rinser has always been aware of the myriad factors that contribute to any event or decision, and in later life she has become even more open to the idea that much is beyond our control and understanding. In her autobiography, *Saturn auf der Sonne* (1994; The Sun in Saturn), she suggests that we leave off questioning, since "life eludes any analysis." She also feels that questions of "guilt" in this life are unwise, since "everything that happens is determined by karma." These are strong arguments for not adopting a judgmental approach to the characters Abelard, Heloise, and Astrolabe. What was right and what was wrong can be endlessly reinterpreted. The weight of the story lies in what was.

Rinser worked on *Abelard's Love* from the end of June 1989 until May 1990. She explains that the impetus for writing the novel was threefold. First, she found a striking similarity between Abelard's emphasis on thought in his inaugural lecture at the Sorbonne and the Jesuit Karl Rahner's emphasis on thought in a lecture delivered in Innsbruck in 1962. Rahner had a more receptive audience; in the twelfth century it was considered heresy. Second, Rinser was fascinated from a feminist standpoint by the "emancipated" Heloise, a lone female whose work was respected in the male academic world. Third, Rinser has always been interested in those who have a great love that remains unfulfilled. The rich texture of the novel raises more issues, among them an adopted child's obsession with birth parents, the type of institution that Roman Catholicism has become, and the balance between one's public and private life.

There is an ebb and flow to the pace of *Abelard's Love* that becomes particularly noticeable to the translator. Quick-moving sections of dialogue are contrasted with weighty philosophical debate. The book gains momentum as Astrolabe becomes more personally involved with his father and introspection gives way to action. Gathering force, it progresses rapidly to its dramatic conclusion. As noted by the reviewer for the German weekly *Welt am Sonntag*, who is quoted on the cover of the German paperback edition, the plot of *Abelard's Love* is developed in a virtuoso manner.

Rinser is one of the most prolific and widely read contemporary German authors. Some of her works have been translated into twenty-two languages. The prizes for literature that she has been awarded include the René Schickele Prize (1952), the Christophorus Book Prize (1975), the Italian National Prize for Literature (Premio Europa; 1980), the Johannes Bobrowski Medal (1985), the Heinrich Mann Prize (1987), the Elizabeth Langgässer Prize for Literature (1988), the Ignazio Silone International Prize for Literature (1991), and most recently the Herkomer Prize.

ACKNOWLEDGMENTS

My thanks to Luise Rinser for entertaining my questions and to outside reader Jeanette R. Clausen and copyeditor Ingrid Muller for their helpful suggestions. At Memorial University, librarian Christopher Dennis ordered any book I needed; classics professor Raymond Clark kindly checked and translated the Latin passages; and student Nicole Gosse wrote her honors essay on Rinser. Our discussions have been mutually beneficial. Above all, my thanks to my husband, Jim, who was always available for consultation. His classically oriented liberal education from the Sisters of Mercy and the Jesuits and his fine feel for style have helped resolve many ambiguities.

Jean M. Snook

❀❀❀❀❀❀❀❀❀❀❀❀❀❀❀❀❀❀❀❀❀❀❀
❀   ❀

Abelard's Love

❀❀❀❀❀❀❀❀❀❀❀❀❀❀❀❀❀❀❀❀❀❀❀❀
❀   ❀

TO MY MOTHER, HELOISE

The package that I delivered unrecognized at the entrance of your convent contains the story of my relations with Peter Abelard, formerly your husband and my procreator, and only now, after his death, really my father. It is the story of the two of you, but more the story of my suffering because of the two of you who brought me into the world in the mad excess of your love, but then pushed me off on an aunt in Brittany, who was considered my mother and who behaved toward me in a more motherly fashion than have you, my real mother. I didn't count in your lives. Overshadowed by you two great figures and your important tasks, I disappeared into nothingness. And yet in the days when you knew you were pregnant by Abelard, you were jubilant, not thinking of the consequences for your child. Even then, in your womb, I was only evidence of Abelard's love to you, not a person in his own right. I was never anyone on my own.

I have tried desperately to free myself from the two of you. In vain; everywhere I went I came upon the deeply engraved trail of Peter Abelard, and next to his ran yours. I've hated you, worshipped you, admired you, despised you, cursed you, envied you, loved you, and all in wild alternation. All my strength was consumed in the effort to get things sorted out with the two of you. The word *father* burned on my tongue and didn't cross my lips. I can speak it now, but it still tastes bitter.

When I heard of the serious illness of Peter Abelard, that is, of my father, I rode immediately to Cluny. Too late. He had died the previous day. Abbot

Peter the Venerable, his friend, your friend, and my friend, led me to him and uncovered his face. Admittedly, age, illness, and all the sorrows and passions of his life had left deep lines, but his face was beautiful – in death even more beautiful than in life. It was the face of my grandfather, his father: the face of an austere knight. I burst into tears. I cried for hours and was so shaken that Peter feared for my health. Peter said I didn't stop repeating the word *father* through my tears. I knew I had lost something irretrievable. I didn't think of what you lost, Mother. That wasn't my business at the time. I am certain that you, too, thought only of your own loss. When I calmed down somewhat, Peter told me, in order to comfort me who cannot be comforted, what a model life my father had led: how he, the most senior person next to the abbot, bore the respect accorded him by all the monks with deepest modesty, almost unwillingly (which of course could also be an expression of his weariness of life, and also of his indifference toward the opinion of those who couldn't appreciate his intellectual significance and were therefore "nobody" to him), how unassuming he was in what he ate, what he drank, and what he wore (as he always had been; these ordinary things had never interested him, he was basically an ascetic and trained in poverty), how he still worked even when he was seriously ill (what else does someone do who has done creative, intellectual work all his life?), how devout he was, how penitently he made his confession. Penitently? But what did he confess? His arrogance about his knowledge? His proud contempt for humanity? His ruthless ambition? His unbridled quarrelsomeness? His betrayal of Fulbert, whose house he dishonored when he seduced the young girl who lived there and with her in blind passion fathered a child who later was in his way? That he then forced (yes: forced!) that girl he had seduced to enter a convent? She was so young, beautiful, and highly gifted, and without calling to the convent life. Did he do it so that she would always be exclusively his? Not the bride of God, no, rather his bride, his alone. Peter says he had a beautiful death, a death in peace, "absolved of all his sins. . . ." That may be. Of what help is it to me, the living witness to his sins? Who is absolving him of the sin against you, Mother, and me? Should I not be happy about the picture that Peter painted of him, for my sake, on a gilded ground? That "Confession of Faith" that my father wrote not long before his death reads like a justification forced out of him by an ecclesiastical court. One could almost take it as a recantation of his teachings, in any case as a clever concession, as if he had finally regarded his lifelong spirited attempt to reconcile belief and thought, St. Paul and Aristotle (in which he subscribed much more to Aristotle than to St. Paul) as fallacious.

One can say that when he wrote it, he was an old, sick, broken man who desired nothing more than his peace. I don't believe all that. I suspect that he concealed his true opinion behind smooth words of orthodoxy. Should he, whose sharp dialectics had been feared all his life, now be let down by them? Should he not have been successful in deceiving everyone with great cunning while remaining true to himself? But perhaps it's the other way around: he is retracting none of his ideas, just making things clear, brushing aside misunderstandings. He writes that people were always prejudiced against him for bringing new ideas to philosophy and theology. For the last time he explains his teaching on the Trinity that made so many enemies for him. He cites St. Augustine as an authority, seems conservatively orthodox, and still smuggles in his own teaching.

Is that how a broken, repentant man writes? That is how someone writes who in all bitterness remains true to himself and is sure of what he says because it is in accord with his own system of logical thought. Whoever has ears to hear hears from this document the language of the proud, wily rebel who, albeit with due caution, champions his cause right up to the end and doesn't pretend to be penitent, not even in the face of death. He repented nothing. Not his teaching, not his life. How could he have regretted preaching the truth? It was the task given him by the Paraclete, the Holy Ghost. He obeyed and, for the sake of this task, took all the conservatives' enmity and humiliation upon himself.

If I may permit myself to judge the academic quality of my father's work: What he achieved belongs to the future. With his dialectics he introduced a new epoch of thought and teaching. Whether the content of his contribution was as significant as Peter the Venerable thinks, I do not know. However, my father himself was significant. He was great in goodness and in . . . No, I can't speak of evil or of goodness. He was neither good nor evil. He was simply himself and not to be measured by normal standards.

I doubt whether my father really ended his days in such deep peace. Peter the Venerable let me guess that this peace, if it ever really did exist, was preceded by agonizing fear that, quite some time before his death, led him to write:

> After a lifetime of being driven around like a wretch, I find death really is a gentle transition, and all those who are troubled by the suffering of others can only wish that there would be an end to all the misery.

A strange sentence, when I think that he never once showed remorse for the suffering that he inflicted on you, Mother. Or did he put into Heloise's mouth the words of the poem he once gave me? "Sunt quos oblectent adeo peccata peracta, / ut nunquam vere poeniteant super his . . ."; "There are people who take too much delight in the sins they have committed to ever really feel remorse for them; indeed, the sweetness of this memory of carnal desire is so great that no thought of punishment can suppress it." Although these and the following lines are written in Abelard's handwriting, it seems very strange to me that they are his thoughts; surely he is quoting Heloise:

> Often our Heloise laments
> To me, and to herself:
> If I could not be saved
> Except by regretting having done what I did earlier,
> There would be no hope for me.
> But what was done lives on so strongly in joyous
> Sweetness that the depth of our desire still
> Enfolds me in memory.

Isn't he also speaking for himself? How can that be reconciled with the moral strictness that he required of himself and his monks? It can and it cannot. He would call this, too, "dialectics" and would take upon himself the task, with the help of dialectics, of reconciling the incompatible and of resolving antitheses into harmony on the highest plane.

Thus he also managed in his last letter to profess piously his faith in Christ (and he certainly meant that seriously) and yet not to renounce his love – the love of both of you – for the unchristian Greek antiquity, but rather to place it at the end of his orthodox "Confession of Faith" as an idea essential for him. He didn't speak of heaven and hell, or of demons, devils, and angels. To the disciple of Aristotle, the Greek myths suggested themselves more readily, so that he wrote:

My certainty of salvation is based on this firm (Christian) foundation of faith, so I don't fear Scylla's barking, I laugh at Charybdis's gorge, I don't shudder at the death-dealing sirens' songs. May the waters' whirling waves come raging in, I won't budge. . . .

The image of Odysseus wandering about the seas may have been before his eyes. I am surprised, Mother, that he didn't remember you as a faithful Penelope. But of course that image would be incorrect; he would sooner have called you Penthesilea.[1]

Mother, the thoughts I am writing down here came to me in the nights I kept vigil by my father's bier in Cluny and as I rode, days later, behind the wagon that brought my father's body to your convent. You had asked for your dead lover, and Peter the Venerable granted your wish.

It was a wonderful April day. The countryside was inundated with blossoms. From a distance, I saw the dead man being carried into your graveyard. There he lies, and there you will lie, at his side. The perfect pair. There is no place there for me. Nevertheless, I still have that poem in one of my father's letters with the line: "Heloisa, who is so dear to us." For this word, I forgive him much.

I don't know if it happened with your consent or only according to my father's will that Peter the Venerable handed over to me your correspondence

---

1. According to Homer, Penthesilea was the queen of the Amazons, killed by Achilles. Another account has Achilles killed by her. In 1808, the German author Heinrich von Kleist wrote a tragedy in which the two are lovers. It ends in a murder-suicide. *Trans.*

and Father's "Confession of Faith." Was I just to preserve the package (but for whom?) or to read the pages? Peter placed them in my hands with silent solemnity the day my father died.

I decided I should read them. I read. I read while I kept vigil beside his bier, hidden behind the backs of the praying monks, by the light of a candle that was burning down.

And I decided to give your letters and Abelard's confessio back to Abbot Peter for his safekeeping. I want to be certain that they don't get lost or fall into the wrong hands. They aren't safe with me. I might burn them in one of my fits of rage (which I still get now and then), in order thereby to destroy my own past. So you should know: Your documents are locked away safely in Cluny.

What I am sending you and asking you to read, you yourself can destroy, if you wish. I'm not certain if you have enough strength to experience your past once again in the mirror of the memories of your and Abelard's son. They are hard words from hard times. From different times. I've tried to organize the pages. Impossible. There can't be written order when only wild disorder is described. You'll find some of the pages illegible. I myself can no longer decipher much of it. Some things are only fleeting notes that were later corrected and completed. Some of it I've lost, or I've torn it up and let the scraps drift down the Seine. Some seems to be repetition but is really a later interpretation of earlier thoughts. The facts, unfortunately, are not invented, you know that, but I saw much of it through the distorting mirror of a tormented young person who doesn't yet understand the nature of fate.

What I wrote was not intended for others' eyes. To be sure, I did address you and also Abelard as if I were writing for the two of you. But they were merely conversations with myself. To put it more precisely, they were substitutes for conversations that you never granted me and that Abelard granted me too late.

I wrote down much of it immediately, without thinking it over. I inserted much of it later, from memory.

Some of it will bore you, because it is only the repetition of Abelard's lectures and opinions, which you know. But perhaps it will interest you nevertheless to find out what Abelard's pupil thought about his teacher and his teachings before he knew that his teacher was his father and what he thought when he knew it.

What you hold in your hands as a thick bundle was begun very early; the boy from Brittany had always liked to write, having inherited the love of language from his parents. It was intended as a simple account of my journey. But even this harmless beginning is overlaid with the shadows of early suspicions and fears. The ghosts were always there. In the course of the years, the account turned into an indictment, or rather a desperate attempt to understand fate and to give meaning to my life. I did not succeed in that.

Now, with the death of my father, my life too has passed. With him I lived a short, intense, and, in its own way, magnificent part of my life. It is over. Before me lie empty years. I am sinking into nothingness. Until my death I'll be nothing but a nondescript, unknown canon by the grace of Peter the Venerable, whom you (I know it and thank you for it) asked to get this job for me. I'll fill it with my shadow. No one will wonder about me.

As far as my account is concerned, consider that a young person wrote it, torn and shaken by suffering so intense he was no match for it. Forgive me if I wrong you in some way. But what is that in comparison to the agonies that you and Abelard have imposed on me, your son.

THE ACCOUNT

Half of France knew what I, whom it concerned, didn't know. My parentage was stubbornly kept secret from me. Since I lived far from Paris in Brittany and since those I took to be my parents kept me away from all strangers, I was twelve years old before I had any doubts about my origin. The cause was the teasing remarks my playmates made about my name. How could you give me this name, Mother? Didn't you know that such an unusual name would expose me to ridicule? Who else is called Astrolabe? You can't have considered how many silly contractions and distortions it has given rise to among the rough boys in our neighborhood. Or wasn't it you who wanted to name me that? Was it he again who is my real father, Abelard, whom you obeyed in everything?

Wouldn't it have been better for you to call me after him, my father, your husband? Peter, after him. Fine. Or not fine, no matter. But this other name is poor: Astrolabe. Latin. Who knew Latin in this Breton family? No one, certainly not the ones I called my parents. Good people, but uneducated. Would they have called me Astrolabe? No, no, it was the two of you, my birth parents, highly educated. But is it even a person's name? I went to our local priest, who lived with his books in the tower.

Is there a saint called Astrolabe?

He didn't know of one. He said it was the name of an astronomical instrument used to determine the position of the stars.

Was that all? I kept on: Were you at my christening, did you perhaps christen me yourself?

No, no, I lived in Paris then.

In Paris. And what brought you here?

My superiors. We clerics are not free knights. Some of us are not well liked in Paris.

Why?

Some think too much, others too little.

Did he know something he was keeping secret from me? Today I'm sure of it, back then I let the matter rest. For a while.

But I'm getting ahead of my story.

I want to try to tell you about my trip, although it is difficult for me not to tell right away about my meeting with the man who fathered me. How did I come to start the search when I didn't even know what I sought? What drove me? Who led me, a demon or a guardian spirit? The question remains open.

I was fifteen, and my private tutor, a priest, could teach me nothing more. He said so himself. I asked him questions that he couldn't answer. I remember the one question that obviously dismayed him. What, I asked, came first: the things or the words for them. You see, Mother, I'm not related to my father only by blood: I thought thoughts that he considered fundamental for philosophy. Years later I heard him lecture on that at the Paris university. My private tutor said to my parents, or rather to the people I then took for my parents, The young man should study, he should go to Paris, the best teachers are there.

No, said my foster father, no, not that, for goodness' sake not to Paris, there are other schools.

He said it so vehemently as if something improper had been asked of him. Today I understand his sharp no: He knew that I would learn something there about my parentage. At the time I got furious. Why shouldn't I go to Paris; am I perhaps not clever enough, or will it cost you too much? Well, I'll earn the money myself.

None of that is at issue, said my foster father.

What is at issue?

Paris is a wicked city full of intrigues, full of scandals, full of prostitution. It's easy to get involved in quarrels there and to get into the worst company. Many a person has already been destroyed there.

Many a person! I said, perhaps. But I'm not many a person. I'm me and grown up enough to be able to survive. I will go to Paris.

You won't.

I will.

I'll lock you up until you give in.

You don't know me. Nobody locks me up.

My mother, who wasn't my mother, seldom interrupted a conversation, but now she said, We have no right to hold him back, and we also have no authority to do so.

We don't? he shouted, very angry now. We have neither right nor authority? Well, then, what do we have? Did we bring him up so that he would run away from us? Right into the arms of fate?

Those words were mysterious to me, yet it seems I guessed the truth through seven veils. But my main concern was to ride to Paris. If I hadn't been allowed to do so, I would have ridden off secretly. But they let me go. They even gave me a good horse, my favorite horse, and a mounted servant, and a purse of money. Before I mounted my horse, my foster mother came and said, Whatever happens, you have a home here. And don't believe everything that you hear. There are things that only God comprehends.

What a strange sentence, I thought. I mounted my horse and galloped away.

Free, free, free, I thought, and didn't know I was on the long leash fate held in its hands, as yet quite loosely, but ready to pull me in more tightly.

For a time I rode along in a carefree manner. After all, I was young and enjoyed riding on a good, fast horse. I was happy it was spring, and I looked forward eagerly to new things. Admittedly, I often felt a secret, ill-defined fear. My mounted servant told me that at night when I was dreaming I thrashed around and spoke angrily in Latin, which I never did during the day. He didn't understand what I said, and I myself knew nothing of it in the morning, and my happiness at riding to a foreign place returned.

Strange that I didn't ride to Paris by the most direct, quickest route, but made all sorts of detours. First I was attracted by the name Finistère. The end of the earth. The extreme end of the Breton peninsula before the immeasurable ocean. I wanted to go to the limit. But when I stood there above the cliffs, I knew it wasn't what I had expected and sought. The limit was not in the outer world. Of course not. There was a Benedictine monastery there. For a whole day, lying high above the cliffs, I thought I could go to the limit by becoming a monk. By living ascetically. But why, what for? For God. Who is God? I had been taught to pray, but otherwise God didn't enter my thoughts. I was young, I wanted to live, to live life to the fullest. I walked across the graveyard. The graves of the shipwrecked, of drowned fishermen, of poor farmers, the leaning gray stone crosses on the graves. And the monks' graveyard. The stone crosses with neither name nor date. Silent stones, each one like all the others. No feeling told me that in one of these nameless graves lay my grandfather, the knight Berengar, Abelard's father. Even if I had known of this grandfather, how could I have understood that he, a knight, lay in a monks' graveyard? When I returned there years later I found out that he was indeed a knight, but he didn't enjoy leading the life of a knight. He was a quiet, devout, educated man who liked to study. He lived in Pallet near Nantes. His wife, my grandmother, was called Lucia. They had two sons, one of whom was Abelard, and a daughter, Denise, my foster mother, my aunt. When the children were grown up, my grandfather entered a monastery, and my grandmother a convent. Retreat from the world. What else. In my grandmother's case it was as Denise told me: After her husband had become a monk, she remained alone on their estate. He had simply gone away. He pretended to be called by God. He didn't wish to be encumbered by the estate any more. He called his property "worldly stuff" and threw it at his wife's feet. But she was incapable of managing the property alone. Denise had gotten married. Abelard, already a scholar at an early age, was gone, at that time to a school in Vannes to study with Roscelin of Compiègne. Then my grandmother also abandoned the "worldly stuff" and entered a convent. Denise saw her for the last time when she was called to Pallet for the settling of the inheritance. Abelard came too. He came from Paris. Even at that time, young as he was, he was giving lectures, but not at the cathedral school, he had a school of his own, where students fought to get in. He emptied the other lecture rooms. He was the magnet, irresistible. He was, said Denise, a self-confident, arrogant young man, tolerated no contradiction, and spoke Latin with the lawyer, intentionally or out of habit, so that she and her husband didn't understand anything. That was long before I was born and long before I was Denise's foster child. Denise said, I asked him about life in Paris. He didn't like being asked. He only said, How can one live anywhere but in Paris? The city scintillates with intellectual life. I belong to those who will rise to the top. I'm already high up.

When he said that, Denise reports, she was afraid of him. She said, One who climbs so high can fall down a long way.

He only laughed.

She said, You will make many enemies.

Oh yes, he said, I'll wake the old dunderheads who don't dare to think for themselves. They've been hibernating for years. I'll expose the liars. I'll crush them quite easily under my feet when I dance with wisdom.

Brother, Brother, she said, you blaspheme against God.

He only laughed again. Poor Denise, little, parochial, God-fearing Breton! What do you know of God?

She still tried to warn him about Parisian women. He said, Women are no temptation for me. I am accustomed to asceticism.

Those were his parting words.

The inheritance was divided up as my grandmother wished. The house went to the convent where she lived, half the land went to the monastery where her husband lived (the monasteries had greedy mouths and large bellies), the remaining half went partly to Denise and to Abelard. What Abelard did with his share I don't know. I wish that I, as the legitimate grandson, had received my share. But that was long before I appeared on this earth. Nonetheless, I got nothing later either. My mother had to beg Peter the Venerable to see to it that I didn't starve and to give me an ecclesiastical sinecure. And we had once possessed this wonderful property and these estates. Damned monasteries, damned greed of the church. I, the grandson, was poor and remain poor.

[13]

But who were your parents, Heloise?

No one found that out. Why? You were an orphan. Really? Really, Mother? Were you found on a doorstep where a maidservant had put you? Was it perhaps Fulbert's doorstep? Who would believe that? People believe something else. They believe . . . I remembered Denise's parting words: Don't believe everything you hear. Fine, I don't believe everything. But some things can be inferred. Why did this canon, Fulbert, take such an interest in you? Why did he let you live in his house? Why did he send you to the best schools? Why did he turn you, the seventeen-year-old, into a scholar who knew Hebrew, Greek, and Latin, who read classical literature and wrote philosophical treatises that caused a sensation? And why was he still unsatisfied with your early fame? What were his intentions for you when he gave you the best, the most expensive of all Parisian scholars, this Abelard, as your private tutor? It turned out badly. I'd like to say: It really served Fulbert right – if I hadn't had to take the rap for it all. The devil had a hand in this. He made use of this Fulbert, of this little man.

Tell me, Mother, was he really your father? Did he beget you with a whore? He wasn't the kind of man who goes to whores. Not only because he was a canon, but because he feared for his position at Notre Dame. Parisian walls have eyes, ears, and noses. If you were his daughter, he wouldn't have taken you into his house. That would have been seen as proof of his paternity. Or was his doing it precisely the proof of his innocence, of his naivety? He was indeed naive, for otherwise he wouldn't have brought Abelard into the house.

Poor, stupid, blind Fulbert. Besides he was so ordinary, a puny, unassertive little man. He wouldn't have enticed a woman into bed. But how did he come by Heloise, this extraordinary girl, who was beautiful and intelligent and who acquired such a great education?

Where do you come from, Mother Heloise?

Have you never found out anything about your origin?

Surely you are the child of a forbidden love, I thought, and surely your parents, whoever they are, were very special people, in high positions, who passed on their intellect to their child.

[14]

Is it a twist of fate that repeated itself with my parents? Was a cleric, a priest, or even a bishop or cardinal involved? Who might my maternal grandmother be?

I never found out.

She was certainly not a whore. The girl that you are and were, Mother, carries the blood and spirit of aristocracy. But something made me wonder: Fulbert's insane fury with Abelard after he found out about your love affair. Only a father, who has a special right to do so, would behave so excessively. Only fathers are capable of such infernally poisonous jealousy. Of course it is also conceivable that Fulbert as a man loved his putative niece or ward, the only love of his life, and that he wished nothing more intensely than to touch her. But he didn't dare to on account of the difference in age, among other things (he could be her grandfather). So he had to hate the one who, although he could be her father, did dare to (and how) without hesitation and without this girl offering even the slightest resistance to the robber of her virginity. The hatred of a fatherly, impotent lover for the forty-year-old, so passionately burning, Abelard. But why had he fetched this still young, handsome, famous man into the house? Must he not have known what he brought about there? Was he so naive as to rely on the girl's chastity? Did he believe that aside from scholarly pursuits there could be no room in her for anything so base as sexual love? Did he trust so blindly in Abelard's noble-mindedness? Or was he certain that this ambitious man would not endanger his career for the sake of a woman? Had this strange Breton knight ever had a love affair? Did he go to whores? Did he have a secret mistress? None of that. He lived ascetically. He lived everything that he did to the full: first the asceticism, then the wild passion. And then, yes, then the asceticism again, forced upon him, to be sure, by the castration; but even without that I'm sure he would have lived ascetically again, because he wasn't made for love, but for learning. Mother, forgive me: Did he really love you or was it only to satisfy his ambition to possess you, the beautiful one, the famous one, the untouched virgin? And besides: Just once he gave in to himself, just once he wanted to experience passion and sexual love. Like everything he did, he did this also completely: He possessed you and never left you alone, he just changed the constellation, he sent you to a convent and remained your mentor and gave you orders. Under the mantle of piety and religious responsibility he kept you bound to this day, and you have never tried to break the bonds; you yourself wanted them, with all the fibers of your body and spirit you wanted them. Oh Mother. What he called loyalty was his proud obstinacy. The falcon kept the prey in his talons. But I digress.

Back to Fulbert. When I visited him in Paris, I did so without wanting to, taken along by a fellow student. Fulbert was an old man, almost blind, but still able to speak toothlessly and spitefully about Abelard. I asked myself why he hadn't simply gotten rid of Abelard once and for all back then. He could have found an assassin, for the right price. Nocturnal murders in the dark, narrow streets around Notre Dame were quite common. Would anybody have suspected Fulbert? Abelard had made many enemies. Anyone could be his murderer. But it didn't have to be murder: a defective stair, soapsuds on it, an accidental fall, a fractured skull, a cerebral hemorrhage, and it would have been all over with the all too keenly scintillating intellect.

Why not do it that way? No, precisely not that way. There had to be disgrace, and it had to be obvious. The punishment had to hit Abelard quite literally in the body part with which he had sinned with so much wild desire. Therefore the castration. That was Fulbert's logic and Fulbert's morality. People could know that he was the instigator of the mutilation. Certainly many applauded him. Abelard could have instituted legal proceedings in Rome. He didn't. But who wreaked the same punishment on the culprits? It can hardly have been Fulbert. Abelard had not only enemies; he also had many powerful friends. And it was they who helped him again and again to obtain teaching positions.

Getting back to the account of my journey. Why didn't I take the shortest way to Paris? I wished for nothing more urgently than to arrive there and begin my studies. Why I made so many detours I could not have explained at the time. Today I know I was afraid. But afraid of what? Afraid of the ghosts of the past that lurked there, formlessly, namelessly. In my isolation from the world in Brittany I had of course heard nothing of all that took place there before and after my birth. I didn't even know the name Abelard.

[16]

So first of all I rode to Finistère. The extreme end of our peninsula. The "end of the earth," which it wasn't, but it was a wild, bleak place high above the sea. Just gray cliffs. It was my first time there. I came from the lush, green pastures and the apple orchards of my village. But this place did not have a tree in sight, not even a stunted bush. No green. No moss. The salty air killed everything. I tasted the sea salt sharply on my tongue and felt it in my eyes. There was no one to be seen anywhere. Our horses searched in vain for a tuft of grass. An unpleasant place. I rode along the coast toward Vannes. Once I lost the path and ended up on a small peninsula, a tongue of land with several buildings on it. I took the whole thing for a farm in disrepair, left to fall into ruin. But in the courtyards there were monks running around in dirty robes and among them children, sheep, and pigs. I asked a boy if it was a monastery. He stared at me. Mentally deficient. Another said, Monastery, yes, monastery, no, it's called Saint-Gildas. This paradoxical response stayed in my mind. I had intended to stay the night, but I was nauseated by the dirt and stench. I let the horses rest and sat down on a boulder in the cliffs. The sea below was thundering against the coast. A wicked place.

And I didn't know at the time that years ago Abelard had sat in that very place, abbot of this dilapidated monastery with these unkempt monks. They were exploited by a violent lord of the manor, who owned the monastery and surrounding countryside. It was sparsely populated by a poor, rough race, whose speech was hardly intelligible. Abelard there as abbot. The great scholar among these savages who strangely enough had chosen him as abbot, certainly not in the expectation that he would educate them to lead a life pleasing to God, but more likely in the hope that someone with more authority would come who could force their exploitative lord of the manor to his knees; or perhaps it was only because of an inscrutable agreement between Saint-Gildas and Saint-Denis, which wanted to get rid of Abelard. Be that as it may: Abelard had become an abbot. It was not a position of distinction. Rather a disciplinary transfer intended to be permanent. Banishment. His teaching over and done with.

Why did Abelard go there? Couldn't he refuse? Did he take the monk's oath of obedience so seriously? Or did the task of reforming a degenerate monastery appeal to him? How he overestimated himself when he tried to enforce even a little external discipline. What he achieved was worse than nothing: the hatred of the monks he had disturbed and the enmity of the lord of the manor who feared that Abelard had powerful supporters. The lord of the manor and his adherents threatened him from the outside, the monks from the inside. The threats were crude and directed at his life, or so it seemed to him. The worst of his sufferings was the humiliation inflicted on him by Saint-Denis. And behind Saint-Denis stood a number of enemies, envious people, malicious, powerful conservatives, who considered the reformer an apostate, a heretic. Had he himself not once said he was considering turning his back on Christian countries and going to the heathen? He wrote – (I read it myself) – that he wanted "to live a Christian life in peace and quiet on some subservient mission among the enemies of Christ." I also read the highly dangerous sentence that he trusted the heathen to give him grace, "since after the charges brought against me they do not expect me to be a Christian and could therefore hope I would be one of them." He was considering, so he wrote, "fleeing to Christ among the enemies of Christ." It was in flight that he went to Saint-Gildas. "That is probably how one leaps into the abyss, in blind fear of the threateningly swung sword," he wrote. He fled from death in seeking it. His life in Saint-Gildas must really have been hell for him. Futile suffering. Cut off from everything that constituted his life: teaching. He had become a nobody.

In the account that Peter the Venerable gave me later I read Abelard's words, quoting the Bible: "This person began to build and was not able to finish." Much had been destroyed for him. It seemed as if in Saint-Gildas he had for the first time accounted for his wrongdoings. "I have earned my suffering," he wrote. Good. But he also wrote that his "previous suffering" seemed insignificant to him "in comparison to my present suffering that I recently brought upon myself." His "previous" suffering? The castration? The separation from his beloved? Insignificant suffering? So to him only one thing was significant: the great humiliation, the end of his career? Why doesn't he say clearly to himself: This is the punishment for my unbridled ambition and my diabolical arrogance? And why not: This is the punishment for what I did to my wife and child? Nothing like that. Did he ever think of our suffering? Did he not forbid you, Mother, in one of the letters Peter the Venerable gave me, to suffer, or rather to speak of your suffering? And you obeyed him. You never again mentioned your pain. What inhuman heroes you were!

When I left Saint-Gildas I was riding so quickly that my horse was in a lather and finally began to limp. My groom overtook me only when I was forced to rest because of the horse. Although he himself was a wild rider, he hadn't been able to keep up with me. He said he had thought we were being pursued, as indeed I was. My pursuer was a ghost with no face and no name, and it rode ahead of me. Months would pass before it presented itself to me incarnate and was called Abelard. The fate that connected me to him, at the time unknown to me, led me on a long leash.

It led me away from Saint-Gildas. I continued on in the direction of Paris, but again and again I left the main road and took strange detours, as if I didn't want to arrive in the place that so attracted me.

One night we slept in a dilapidated wooden hut at the edge of a forest. In the morning we were awakened by a man carrying an ax on his shoulder. I reached for my knife, but the old man wasn't going to do us any harm. He was a woodcutter and was surprised to find strange men and horses there. He took us for people who had lost their way, who hadn't been able to find the house they were looking for in the night. What house? We hadn't looked for one. It's a convent, said the woodcutter, it's called "The Paraclete." I heard that name for the first time, and it meant nothing to me. What business did I have there?

The woodcutter said it was famous. The prioress was still young and much too beautiful for a nun. God only knew what caused her to enter the convent. Sometimes a man came on horseback, a monk who preached there, but nobody could say anything bad about that; all the nuns held him in high esteem. He was said to have once been a famous scholar.

Why "have been?" Is he dead?

No one knows anything for certain. But we're sure he was a famous professor in Paris. When he came here the first time, he was alone. He built himself this hut here.

[19]

My God, Mother, just think: I had slept in Abelard's hut! It gives me the shivers.

At first the professor lived alone, I brought him bread sometimes, he lived on almost nothing, I felt sorry for him. (Blessings on you, aged woodcutter!) But then young people came, more and more of them, and built themselves huts like this one here and lived in poverty. I thought they were young monks, but they were students from Paris who had followed their teacher here. You can't imagine how attached they were to him. But all at once strange men came and took him away, not exactly in chains, but as if he were a criminal. The students wanted to fight against the men, but their teacher turned them back. That was all very strange. And then the students scattered to the four winds, so to speak. But one day they came back again, this time alone, and built the stone church there, and then a house, and then the nuns came.

The old man was talkative. I listened to him only out of courtesy. For a moment I wondered if I should go to see the church and the convent. But I rode on.

What would have happened if I had knocked at the convent gate? Nothing. What sensible reason could I have stated for making a visit? To whom? Even if I had known the name of the prioress, nothing would have happened. Or would it? Or perhaps . . . Would mother and son have recognized each other? I don't think so. No, I don't think so. But what if they had?

Nevertheless, I rode on, but after a while I felt a pang, as if I had neglected something important. But I was ashamed to turn around. Ashamed before whom? A strange mood. I got over it by riding like one possessed and thinking continuously of that professor, the students' idol and some sort of criminal. And who were the people who took him away?

Today we know: Alberich and Lotulf, directors of the cathedral school in Reims, Abelard's envious and lethal foes. We also know today where they took him: to the Saint-Médard monastery near Soissons. A monastery, to be sure, but what a monastery: a correctional institution for recalcitrant monks, a lunatic asylum for priests, for those who really were mentally deranged and those whose enemies maintained they were crazy and spreading the teachings of the devil – the institution of a church that stubbornly refused to accept new ideas and people of great character. It is clear into which wing they sent Abelard. In any case, the monastery was a prison. Here the dangerous Abelard was to be silenced. For ever.

But it didn't turn out as his enemies planned. The abbot of the prison monastery respected the great, if highly troublesome and stubborn, scholar Abelard and arranged for him to be brought to the monastery at Saint-Denis. There was and still is a significant library there. Abelard was to work there in peace under the supervision of the abbot.

To work in peace. As if Abelard knew what peace was. It wasn't long before his daemon tormented him again. I heard the story from several sides. Later. Even now I know only parts of it. I could perhaps have heard the story back then if I had ridden to Saint-Denis, and I would have done so if I hadn't been thrown from my horse at a crossroads – for the first time, it was a good horse. But perhaps I had hurried it too much and exhausted it. It shied at a shadow. I sprained my left foot and injured my knee. Whether I wanted to or not, I had to be treated in the next town. The town was Corbeil.

What would I have heard at that time in Saint-Denis? Fate decided it wasn't yet time for me to meet my father. I didn't even know his name yet. I heard it for the first time that evening in the inn.

The innkeeper took me for a student. That flattered me, foolishly, because I wasn't one yet.

But what brings you here to Corbeil; there has been nothing at all going on here since the great Baillardus went away.

The physician who bandaged my leg said, It's a pity about him.

Why?

He was born too early.

What do you mean?

He was a great star in the firmament of learning. But the star is extinguished, it has been extinguished because it shone too brightly. That makes people envious.

Without great curiosity I asked where this star had gone.

The innkeeper didn't know. The physician said, He disappeared one day. He was very ill. A nervous fever. I fear he didn't survive it.

[21]

You mean he is dead?

Only now do I know why I was afraid of the answer. Today, after I had wished him dead for years. After I had stabbed him, poisoned him, choked him many times in my imagination. According to Abelard's reasoning, I am a murderer: The sin lies not in the executed deed but in the intention. This is the theory for which he was declared a heretic. However, I am of his opinion. Nevertheless, I don't feel guilty, because what he did to you, to you and to me, Mother, weighs a hundred times more heavily than a young person's wish to kill, a young person who is himself mortally wounded. I am that selfsame person, Mother: a person with an incurable wound.

At that time, in Corbeil, I feared the physician's answer. But he only said, There are people who survive the fever, but they must be of very strong constitution, and he wasn't, and anyone who lives like that beyond his strength . . .

He simply doesn't survive, I said.

The physician shrugged his shoulders, as would anyone who doesn't want to say directly what he is thinking. Did he know something? What could he know beyond what he had said? Did he know what I know today: this Baillardus was so delicate as a child that his parents decided to let him study, since he wasn't suited for life as a knight. Poor parents or, rather, poor son of those parents, who could not guess what fate they determined for him. What must they have thought when he, not yet thirty years old, came home suffering from a nervous disease and on the verge of madness. What did they know of this son? What news came from Paris to Pallet? In any case, they received him with open arms and cured him, who knows how, presumably just by leaving him in peace and making no demands on him. No one else knew his whereabouts. For Paris, Melun, Corbeil, for the world of knowledge, for friends and enemies he was a dead man.

"While I had to stay away from France for a few years, the young students missed me sorely," he wrote in his *Story of My Misfortunes*. What did he do during that time? He wrote nothing; in any case, not a line has been preserved. Perhaps he plotted revenge on his enemies, perhaps he just brooded by himself and let his highly overwrought mind have a rest among apple trees,

[22]

sheep, horses, and peaceful people. Did it never occur to him that his illness was a warning signal of fate? That he would have to atone for his diabolical arrogance? That he should recognize his limits? Did he learn something in these years? He learned nothing. Scarcely recuperated, he plunged into the battle all over again.

He turned up again in the middle of the enemy camp. It seemed as if they had never reckoned on his death, but had awaited his return. The activity at the university was unthinkable without him. Without him, everything was dry as dust. The students flocked around him, the magician, the daredevil reformer.

A hundred times I think, If only he hadn't come back. If only he had died. If only nothing remained of him but a stone cross in the graveyard in Pallet, much weather worn already, the name now barely legible: Peter Abelard, born 1079, died 1109. To think of all that wouldn't have happened. Fate wouldn't have set an insoluble task. Two important people wouldn't have fallen victim to this ill-starred passion, I wouldn't have been fathered, I wouldn't have been condemned to this life that is nothing but suffering. You, Mother, wouldn't have been forced to enter the convent, so young, beautiful, and talented. And Abelard wouldn't . . .

The physician had said, "It's a pity about the man." I remembered that. But who said, It's a pity about his son? No one. Not a soul. I am a person of limited intellect. A nobody. A shadow in the shadow of a great father. Who said, It's a pity about Heloise? Oh, many said that, to be sure. When she took the veil, "voluntarily," no, not voluntarily, many people cried. When Abelard entered the monastery at Saint-Denis, no one cried but you, Heloise. But perhaps you didn't cry, strong woman that you are.

Abelard as a monk. Abelard no longer the great teacher of philosophy. Abelard obliged to obey orders, without freedom of thought. That could not turn out well. Nothing went well. Nowhere and never. It had already begun in Paris when Abelard himself was little more than a student. His teacher was famous, William of Champeaux. The young Abelard was provoked by the famous man's self-confidence and the apparent incontestability of his theses. What got into him when he began to argue with his teacher? That was unheard of. A spectacle for the students. The young man was a match for the famous old man in keenness of logical thinking and in eloquence. Now and then he got the old man rattled, and the teacher had to admit he was beaten. What professor tolerates that? William was interested in the highly gifted student, but only in the beginning, then he began to hate him, at first secretly, then openly, and naturally he had those students on his side who were annoyed at this very bright, impertinent fellow student. Things did not go well for long. They never did go well for long with Abelard: he preferred to leave the battlefield of Paris and to found a school himself. That was audacious. William found out about it and did his utmost to prevent it. But Abelard had powerful friends. Who his helpers were I don't know. Naturally enemies of William. The enemies of the one, the friends of the other. That too belongs to the pattern of Abelard's life. It is also pertinent that although he wasn't physically strong, he was endowed with such dogged stubbornness that he achieved what he wanted: he got his school in Melun, and he got his students, oh yes, he was at that time already the magnet attracting the young people. They simply came under his spell. When Melun got too provincial for him, he moved closer to the capital, to Corbeil, and the students moved with him, and many others left Paris to go to Corbeil. Abelard was all the rage. The star was shining, but its brilliance was a strong challenge to the Parisian professors. At first that appealed to him beyond all measure: to have so many great enemies proves that one is significant.

It's a pity about the man, he was born too early.

What was the physician trying to say? When one says of someone that he was born too early, then one wants to say that he was ahead of his time. But one who is ahead of his time is not understood and is conveniently declared to be a dangerous revolutionary and a heretic who ought to be destroyed in the interest of the existing order, in the interest of the power of the high and mighty.

Abelard had not underestimated his enemies, but overestimated his own strength: he got sick. After his return he taught at first in Laon. He taught philosophy, to be precise, dialectics. But he also taught theology. How did that come about? He had never studied theology. They provoked him: they presented him with a difficult, unclear passage from Ezekiel, about which he was to speak freely, and they gave him time to prepare, as is fitting. Again the devil of arrogance possessed him: he did not need to do routine work. He himself wrote that he said: "I rely on my genius." He spoke freely and without any preparation about an exegetical problem that was new for him, and he fascinated his audience. Soon his exegesis lectures were filled to overflowing. Is it surprising that his enemies loathed and detested him, especially one of his former teachers, Anselm of Laon? He forbade him to teach in Laon.

He had not reckoned with Abelard's students: they were furious with Anselm. They rebelled. They stood firmly by Abelard, and when he had to leave Laon, they went with him. He always had the young people on his side. He was always the cause and focus of great disputes. And he always lashed out, and he always suffered and made others suffer. And he always had great victories to record, but he always paid dearly for them. He didn't consider, at least at that time, that others were also paying the bill of fate. He was obsessed with himself. A person defiled by his own daemon. I know and say that today for the first time, and if you've read to this point in my account, Mother, then you'll understand the route by which I have come from sheer hatred and the wish to murder him to an agonizing understanding of this peculiar man who is my father.

At that time, after his return from Laon to Paris, he experienced a few peaceful years. He was offered a chair at the university, which he of course accepted. He was famous, very famous, he had the most students and earned a lot from the lecture fees. And he was appointed canon of Notre Dame, an honor he would have done better not to accept, because associated with the honor was the obligation, albeit not of monastic chastity, of celibacy.

How could Abelard think he would ever enter into marriage? And that, when he wanted to, his beloved would resist, because she did not want him to lose his position and damage his career? How could he think he would almost have to fight with her for her consent to marriage and that this astounding young girl Heloise would rather remain his "whore" (so she wrote) than destroy his career? The marriage took place. So I am a legitimate child. Oh yes. All legal. Everything in perfect order. Except that the legitimate child, fathered premaritally, lustfully, knew nothing of it. Eighteen years went by before this child, grown into a young man in remote Brittany, discovered who his legal parents were and why he nevertheless hadn't been allowed to have parents. His mother a nun, his father a monk. Admittedly, they were far from that when they brought him into the world. In those days they were a couple caught up in the madness of love and had no thought for the consequences. Thus I came into being. A love child, indeed, a child of blind passion. The child of two great, famous people. Shouldn't I be proud of it? Wasn't I a hundred times happier when I could consider myself the child of a Breton couple who did some farming? Hadn't I forced my fate myself? Didn't I want to go to Paris at any cost? Didn't I voluntarily play into its hands? Didn't the black thread unwind of its own accord? No one escapes his fate. As I write this, Mother, I am telling you that, logically, I can't find the two of you guilty. Of course that doesn't stop my suffering and blaming you against my deeper insight. Because am I not a eunuch like my father? He was one literally and through physical mutilation. I'm one through the mutilation of my soul. He could no longer love physically, I cannot either; I am hindered by fear, but not fear of losing my job as canon, the job that I know Peter the Venerable procured for me at your request; it is fear of myself. Fear that I could let myself be driven by a passion like yours. I am afraid of women. I'm young and well built, and the Parisian girls cast glances at me. I burn to be with them, but remain outwardly cold; through all the years I've remained an irreproachable student, an irreproachable canon amid all the temptations. But those nights! Things were merry in the streets and in the pubs. People sang. Mother, they sang the love songs that your beloved wrote for you, the words and music. I didn't know it. How could I have known it: no one knew the name of the author. It was "some troubadour." Any of them. A minstrel celebrating his lady in song; she was anyone, no one in particular, but simply "the lady."

Once I heard such a song close by. A girl sang it. The words were difficult to understand: corrupt Latin. I dared to speak to the girl and ask about the words. The song is about Jephthah's daughter, she said; it's a long song, a whole story, a sad one. Who is this Jephthah? The girl didn't know; it was just a story. I knew: The name Jephthah appears in the Old Testament, in

[26]

the Book of Judges. Jephthah takes a vow: "God, if you let me vanquish the Ammonites, then the first thing that steps out the door of my house and comes to meet me is yours; I will present it to you as a burnt offering." He returns home victorious. The first to greet him is his daughter, singing and dancing. It breaks his heart. The girl, however, is strong. One must keep one's promises to God. She asks for only one thing: a two-month reprieve, so that she can roam through the mountains with her girlfriends and weep. In the text it says, "She wept over her virginity." A strange word: Had she lost her virginity? No. She came back a virgin and was sacrificed by her father. Placed on the altar as a burnt offering, like a lamb – "as he had solemnly promised." But why those tears? Was she weeping over her fate that condemned her to be a virgin and didn't allow her to experience love? Why did she actually return from the mountains to her death? Was she unable to flee? She was unable to because she was the chosen sacrificial lamb that her father had promised to his God.

I asked the girl to sing me the song again and again, not because it was so beautiful, which of course it was, but rather because it preoccupied me so. What a cruel father. What a cruel God, who didn't stay his arm as he sacrificed his daughter. What strength in the girl, what saintly obstinacy. Today I know why that song haunted me so. The sacrificed girl: Heloise. The father: Abelard. The sacrifice: He sent Heloise to the convent.

A difference: Jephthah's daughter lay down voluntarily on the pile of wood to be burned. And Heloise? Voluntarily? At one time I wanted to believe that. It is different, altogether different, Mother: Your Jephthah dragged you by force to the sacrificial stone, but you let yourself be dragged defenselessly and gave the appearance of going voluntarily. Difficult to understand: voluntarily and yet forced, that is a dialectic that I just barely understand. What I don't understand is that you haven't really come to terms with it your whole life long. In letters to the priest who sacrificed you, you bitterly reproached him. And at the same time loved him, constantly, passionately, and in torment. Out of love for your lover, who was your lawful husband, you entered the convent. Out of love you had not wanted to marry him. Out of love you would have preferred to be called his whore. All out of love. But why then

[27]

the violent and bitter complaints? Had you demanded too much of yourself by "voluntarily" becoming a nun for Abelard's sake when you were so young and beautiful and had such a talent for love? Your letters from the convent are such that had one of your nuns written them, you as prioress would have had to expel her from the convent. Blasphemous letters. Through Abelard you are accusing God. Abelard had written to you that you should pray for him. That, however, was what you couldn't do, because what was he to you, the God you should pray to? There was only one God for you: Abelard, Abelard, Abelard. But precisely this God was father Jephthah: He held his sacrificial lamb firmly on the sacrificial table with glowing chains. The bound lamb screamed. It called to its God:

I have only one solace in this world: you. Pleasing you is closer to my heart than pleasing God. My taking the veil was not out of love for God, it was only at your command. So I can have no hope of thanks either in this world or the next. I am the poorest of the poor, the unhappiest of the unhappy. You had lifted me up, you brought honor on me above all women, and high though I climbed, I fell just as far, fell because of you and me at the same time. Of all women not one was so favored by fate that she could stand above me or even at my side. Therefore, there was no one else fate could fling down so far and let be so consumed with sorrow. Fate also gave me some of the glory of your fame; with your fall it stole it back from me. Fate has given me both good and bad fortune in excess. In order to be able to exaggerate the sorrow of my love, it first exaggerated the bliss of my love.

That is what you wrote, Mother. When you wrote it, you were twenty years old, as old as I am now. I ask myself if you don't exaggerate, infected with Abelard's art of rhetoric, when you write of him that he is the greatest philosopher of his time and he has lifted you up to himself. Weren't you someone yourself, weren't you already famous yourself for your great knowledge, weren't you admired by many, even by Peter the Venerable, who, I suspect, loved you? Wouldn't it be true to say that it was you who first made Abelard what he was? Didn't you make him a man, the wild boy Abelard? Weren't you the instrument of fate when he plunged into love and into sin? Didn't you tear open the curtain of vanity and self-confidence that had separated him from real life? Weren't you the greater one, Mother? You were certainly the greater in love.

But I've gotten too far ahead of myself. Back to Corbeil. Hardly was my foot healed enough for me to mount my horse than I rode to Paris.

There it lay before me. No shining Jerusalem. No cosmopolitan city of one's dreams like Rome or in times past Byzantium or Alexandria or even Athens. Rather a heap of houses strewn across the landscape, crowding against a center that forms the city. Dirty, narrow streets, suspicious-looking inns, stray dogs, and howling cats. Disorder everywhere. Did I want to stay here? I was already homesick for Brittany, for the sheep pastures and apple orchards and my family. Here I was alone. But go back? No. I found a place to stay, put my horse in the stable, and sent the servant with his horse back to Pallet.

My life as a student began an hour later. It began with a scene that to me was completely incomprehensible. A group of young people was standing in the square of Notre Dame. Students. They were heatedly discussing something. I heard Abelard's name. I was too shy to join them. But they called me. They asked what I was going to study. What indeed? Did I know? I said: Philosophy.

You came because of Abelard?

What a question. I didn't even know who this Abelard was. They noticed that I came from the country. A farmer among students. One of the young men immediately appointed himself my tutor and took me along with him.

Where?

To Fulbert.

Who's that?

A skeleton for the medical students to study.

Do be serious!

I am. He's an evil old man. Canon of Notre Dame. He has a few things on his conscience.

What, for instance?

Later.

What's there for me to do?

You're just coming with me; I have to return a book to him. It'll only take a few minutes.

[29]

We climbed a steep flight of stairs. Do you remember them, Mother? And Fulbert's study? Stale air. Dust on the furniture. He himself was truly a skeleton who almost disappeared in the armchair. My tutor put the book on the table and wanted to go. Fulbert asked, Who is that with you?

My tutor whispered to me, He's almost deaf and almost blind. He said aloud, This is a new student, still a stranger here.

Come closer, you. Still closer. Where do you come from?

From Brittany.

So. Where in Brittany?

What kept me from mentioning the name Pallet? I said another one. Any name. One I made up.

Fulbert leaned forward. Come closer. What color are your eyes?

A curious question. They're gray, I said and lied. This interrogation annoyed me. It went on.

Who are your parents?

A nobleman from the country. He is dead.

I thought, Why the hell am I lying?

You speak a dialect I know. Are you from Nantes?

No.

That was not a lie.

How old are you?

Again I lied. Seventeen. I was eighteen.

I saw that the old man was doing a calculation; he used his fingers for it. Then he sighed as if relieved.

On with the interrogation: What are you studying?

Nothing yet.

The best thing for you to study would be nothing at all. What is taught in our universities today is useless. Stuff of the devil. The modern teachers are heretics. Probably you even want to study with the chief heretic? With that disgraceful whoremonger, Abelard? And you there, are you studying with him too?

Yes, said my tutor; he's the best teacher we have.

[30]

An explosion. Fulbert, weak as he was, sprang to his feet. Get out, both of you! Get out!

We went.

My tutor said, Poor man, he can't get over it.

Over what?

He hates Abelard because of his fame.

But why whoremonger? That's a bit much.

People say Abelard had a love affair with Fulbert's ward, and for that he had Abelard emasculated.

Emasculated?

Well, aren't you from the country?

And?

You have your oxen castrated when you don't want bulls.

I don't understand you.

It doesn't matter. Perhaps it's all just gossip. You don't know yet that Paris is a viper's nest. People gossip about everyone and everything. But believe me: Abelard is a wonderful teacher. Very modern. He teaches us logical thought. That opens our eyes and ears. That kind of philosophy is new. But he also teaches theology. He says, Thinking and believing must be in agreement. One must grasp them through thinking. Thinking for oneself. Not parroting of established theorems. He demands a lot. His exams are the most difficult. He simply doesn't let anything stand that one hasn't thought through completely. What do you think, for example, about the question: What came first, the things or their names?

I think both belong together; therefore they were both there at the same time.

Holy simplicity. The way you just say that, in all naivety. The scholars argue about it, and you just say it like that.

Yes, but the things are also there if one doesn't give them names. But names that don't describe anything are impossible.

The question is, What was there first, do you understand?

No. Not at all. But if that is what one learns at the university, then . . .

[31]

Don't talk now. Come to Abelard's lecture tomorrow. It's the introductory lecture.

I was in the large lecture hall on time; it was the largest in the university. When I arrived, it was already full. Also full of noise. Suddenly stillness. Then shouting, shouts of joy, and trampling. The students stood up to greet the professor. At the time I thought that was the custom. It wasn't the custom. Then it got quiet. A raised hand made a sign and all sat down wherever they could find a place. That hand, that sign: it was authoritarian.

Then I saw him: Abelard. The tide of students had pushed me to the front. So I saw him up close.

Did I have any idea what this man was to me? I stared at him. He resembled my grandfather Berengar, the knight who became a monk. A sign was given to me. Too early. What was he talking about? I heard words but found no coherence. I heard "nominalism," "universalism," "logic," "dialectic" . . .

He spoke a beautiful Latin, like my private tutor in Pallet, who was a Parisian, but sometimes I heard an intonation that seemed familiar to me. He isn't a born Parisian, I thought. But I didn't think further. I stared at him. A handsome man, really. No longer young. Over fifty, I later heard. Tall and well built. A sharp-featured face. When he paused for a moment, I noticed that his closed mouth was hard and bitter. Thick, gray, somewhat tousled hair. Again and again, as his speech became animated, a strand of hair fell across his face. He pushed it back nervously. That hand fascinated me. Now and then he knocked on the lectern with his knuckles. A hard rap. A closing point. Authoritarian. It bothered me. It was in contradiction to his words that the students had previously greeted with applause: One must recognize no authority but think for oneself. What a statement! Revolutionary. But this hard knocking with his knuckles. For the first time I encountered what made Abelard so many enemies: this colossal claim to absolute respect for his views and his method. But the same students whom he taught to rebel against everything conservative and authoritarian clung to him, the great authority, as if they were bewitched. So did I. I felt my displeasure at that hard rapping melt away. I resisted. I wanted to remain critical. As he required of us: be critical, think for yourself. But where should my criticism have begun? I still understood next to nothing of his lectures, although my private tutor in Pallet was a very good one and was also modern. But this Abelard: What must he have been like when he was young? What kind of impression must he have made then on the Parisian women, this handsome, masculine, arrogant man, this foreign knight, this aristocrat, this Breton bird of prey?

Women pursued him, I heard later. They tried to catch him. He despised them. He wrote in his *Story of My Misfortunes* that I got to read much, much later:

I always had a natural abhorrence of dirty intercourse with prostitutes; there was never an occasion for social relations with women of the aristocracy because I was always completely preoccupied with my lectures; I didn't have the right social skills for the middle-class girls.

No love affairs then. Only his studies, only his lectures, only the desire to know and to understand. Only the ambition to be the greatest of all contemporary philosophers and later the greatest of theologians. Incidentally, he never achieved that: The theologians didn't take him seriously, he was too much of a philosopher, he straddled the fence between the two disciplines. But his own position was of course very high up. There was no room for a woman in that life. Chastity not out of virtue but out of arrogance.

Until the one woman came along.

"At that time a girl called Heloise lived in Paris."

I read it in Abelard's *Story of My Misfortunes*.

A girl, Heloise. My mother. My unknown mother.

I saw my father almost every day without recognizing him as my father. I was an enthusiastic student. I soon grasped what mattered to my teacher: rational thought and speech. He had thrown the igniting spark among us in the first lecture. The topic was "On the Divine Unity and Trinity." Abelard supported the scholarly claim of being able to make the incomprehensible comprehensible.

Until then I had heard nothing other than that one had to "believe." My private tutor, who had already had a taste of the new Paris dishes, didn't dare to educate me in Abelard's sense. However, I remembered him saying that

[33]

one fell into disrepute in Paris if one thought too much. Hadn't he given me to understand that he'd been sent to the country, and thus put out of the way, precisely because he had thought too much, too independently? Could it be that he wanted to make a devout believer out of me? Why? Because he wanted to protect me from a fate similar to his own? Or because he had laid down the weapons of the intellect in view of the dangers that one conjured up when using them?

But now Abelard: he thought, and he required us to think. It was senseless to parrot memorized material; words that gave one nothing to think about were superfluous, indeed pernicious. Even in theology. One couldn't speak of belief until one knew the meaning of what one said. Always the question: What does one actually mean when one says, for example, Jesus is the Word Incarnate. What does one actually mean . . . At first I was shocked: He is undermining the ecclesiastical faith, he is rejecting the *sacrificium intellectus* that the church demanded, he is denying every conservative theological thesis, he is actually attacking the whole corpus of accepted theology. Belief, he said, is nothing magical and nothing occult. Belief is the fruit of the agreement between one's own reason and the teaching of the church. But, I thought, what if one can't believe that way, because what one is supposed to believe is absurd? A question of interpretation, as I gradually learned from Abelard. One must tackle theology with the means of philosophy, one must use logic and dialectics. I began to understand that he was not attacking belief in itself, but the fear of also wanting to understand belief with the intellect. But, I thought, aren't there many things in the world that one cannot grasp with reason, but only with the help of another mental power? But which one? I found no word for it; "imagination" presented itself, but that was an altogether unscholarly term. Has Abelard recognized everything he thinks through thinking? Isn't his thinking just the visible aspect of his believing? If he hadn't previously "believed," then he would have had nothing about which he could think. A variation of the question: What was first, the name of an object or the object; the thing or the concept one has of it; the real thing or the idea? Everything came down to whether one considered Plato or Aristotle to be right, and Augustine too, whom Abelard frequently quoted.

[34]

His lectures on the Trinity were difficult to understand. I must confess that they didn't much interest me. They wouldn't have interested me at all if I hadn't been tested on them in the exam. And, I must add, I would also have had to feel guilty if I had considered something unimportant that was so essential to Abelard. I took it as practice in logic.

The exam. The first time that I stood right in front of Abelard. I had seen him many times behind the lectern. He had never noticed me in the throng of his students. I well knew what he would ask me. I had studied the matter well: Was Arianism a heresy and, if so, to what extent?

It is a heresy, I said, in so far as it maintains that God's son is not of the same substance as the Father, but only resembles him; that the Word is God only because it is part of the substance of God, exactly like all human beings; that it is not the second person in the Trinity; that the Holy Ghost is, like the Father and the Son, a hypostasis distinct from the other two. . . . I rattled off my knowledge. Suddenly I noticed that he was looking at me sharply. That's enough, he said. I bet you don't understand a word of what you're saying, and the matter is unimportant to you.

He confused me. He continued to look at me sharply while he went on questioning me. Now he led me out onto thin ice: he asked about the dispute between the universalists and the nominalists. I knew that Abelard, as a student of Roscelin, taught universalism, without committing himself to either of the two extreme schools of thought. Therefore I said what I thought he wanted to hear: There is a *universale transcendentale* and a *universale praedicabile*.

Abelard interrupted me. Say it in your own words!

The problem is: Is there something common or identical in everything that exists, and what is its nature? Is it something ideal, as Plato teaches, or something real, as Aristotle teaches? Philo teaches that universal ideas are contained in the Divine Word. Augustine sees ideas as divine thoughts that are models for all kinds and types of things. The question is whether universals are only concepts or are indeed real things, and whether concepts are only words. . . .

He interrupted me again. Don't answer with superficially acquired knowledge, but with your own views.

[35]

But my views are unimportant and probably wrong.

Abelard got impatient. Answer!

A leap into cold water, or rather into fire. I certainly wouldn't pass the exam. Now it was immaterial what I said.

Well, I believe that neither the nominalists nor the universalists are right. I believe there is the one and the many. The one is in everything and expresses itself in diversity. Existence in itself . . .

Abelard interrupted me. Say that again.

What, existence in itself?

Where did you get that?

It just came to me.

Continue.

Existence in itself and the names people give it to distinguish between its manifold aspects don't seem to me to be a contradiction.

What came first, the real thing or its name? Say it in your own words!

In the beginning was the Word, it says. But what is that, the beginning? When one speaks of a beginning, one makes the assumption that there is time, as if time for God had a beginning, and as if there were a time before, during, and after the creation. But the creation was in God without beginning as an idea, and every thing was already named by God. He said: Let there be light. Then light was really there, but it was already previously there in God. The difference between things and their names is a human way of thinking. I think one can understand the *sic et non* that way.

Abelard looked at me in a way that made me fear I had said something foolish or even (in his sense) heretical.

Continue!

What should I say?

You spoke about God. What do you know about God?

Nothing, because one cannot know anything about him, not even what he is not. He would only be recognizable by someone who was outside of him. But no one is outside of him. So who could know him?

You want to say that neither philosophy nor theology is of any use in knowing God?

[36]

I was silent.

He said, Why are you studying philosophy and theology if you think they aren't of any use in knowing God?

I didn't say that these subjects don't help one to know. They teach one how to think. In astronomy one learns something about the sun, but if I look at it, I am blinded and see only darkness.

So for you God is light?

That's an image; I can't think of any other. I could also say he is darkness.

Abelard looked at me in a frightening way. Then he said, You know something of Plato and of Aristotle. But you are, although you don't know it, a follower of the mystic Dionysius the Areopagite. Have you heard of him?

No, never.

One final question: What do you think about freedom of will? Is one free to choose between good and evil?

I didn't know what to say to that, and Abelard stood up brusquely.

Wait for me tomorrow after the lecture.

Had I passed the exam or not? I remained behind, distraught. Had it even been an exam? This strange professor wasn't interested in any of the things I had learned so assiduously. And he hadn't even asked about his hobbyhorse, or rather his war horse: the Trinity and the position of the Paraclete, the Holy Ghost, in that Trinity. I had been prepared for it. Now I could forget it. So I thought. It turned out differently. That word "Paraclete" became a knife with which fate stabbed me again and again. Father, Son, and, yes, the Paraclete. The name of the convent where my mother lives as a nun. The other Trinity: Abelard, Peter Astrolabe, Heloise. The distorted, blasphemous image remains burned into me.

At that time, after the exam, Abelard's gaze haunted me for months. How he had stared at me again and again and then turned his head away with a jerk as if he didn't want to see me any more or as if he suddenly heard something that startled and distracted him or called him away to another activity. He was nervous. He always was, but this time he was nervous in a special way.

And how was I? Didn't I feel anything special? Didn't my heart beat more rapidly? Didn't I suspect anything? Absolutely nothing. I was concentrating

[37]

strictly on the exam, not knowing whether I had passed it or not. My fellow students were waiting for me. They wanted to know what I had been asked. I said, About the dispute between the nominalists and universalists, and naturally about the Trinity.

Did you pass?

I don't know.

He must have told you.

I'll find out tomorrow.

Of course you passed. Let's go for a drink.

I had nothing to celebrate yet. And I couldn't stand taverns, couldn't stand the wine and certainly not the girls who sidled up to me there. But I went along. That evening I heard one of them sing the song I had already heard once on my first day in Paris. Now I understood the text.

O girl, the rare strength of your soul awakens
Wonderment and mourning in us simultaneously.
For you said, girl:
May heaven be willing
That my innocence make me worthy
To offer myself as a sacrifice.

*

Don't waver, Father, in body or in mind, I beg you.
Don't forgo your fame or mine.
Don't value my life more highly than your genius. . . .

It's the song of Jephthah, said one of my fellow students.

I said, But that's no ordinary song, and the poet was no ordinary troubadour. That's no love song. I'd like to know what it means.

I told you: It's the song of Jephthah and his daughter, who was sacrificed. . . .

I know. But the words aren't at all appropriate for Jephthah and his daughter. Don't value my life more highly than your genius. That doesn't make any sense in the old story. Someone wanted to say something else

[38]

there. Who is meant by Jephthah and who by his daughter? And who is the poet?

Someone said, He's anonymous.

But surely one can find out who he is. It's a matter of stylistic analysis (one of Abelard's expressions).

Why are you so interested in it?

Why I am so interested in it, yes, why? Don't value my life more highly than your genius. The daughter says that to her father, who has made a careless vow? How does that go together?

So the next day I waited for Abelard. What did he want from me? Did he want to continue the exam? Was he still uncertain whether to fail me or not?

We were alone.

Have you given any more thought to the Trinity and the Paraclete?

No, I said, and suddenly I was angry. He was tormenting me. Could I suspect that he was tormenting himself mercilessly? He looked worn out, he was much more nervous than usual and made me nervous too.

Why don't you tell me that I failed?

You didn't fail.

But why . . .

I asked you a question.

Yes, but my answer may be a heresy.

Everything is a question of interpretation.

Well, I have an image of three candles. One can take each one by itself; one can also hold all three candles together so that there is a single flame. But one can also take them by themselves again. The one flame is in all three in like manner, and yet each is something in itself.

Abelard looked at me penetratingly again. That's a poetic image, he said. You have a feeling for imagery and poetry. Poets don't become great philosophers and theologians. They don't think, they look.

Had I been a few weeks older, I could have answered him sharply, You too, Abelard, were once a poet, a troubadour indeed. You wrote love songs. They were many, beautiful. You canceled your lectures. And yet you have become what you are. But I didn't yet know that at the time of this encounter.

[39]

Quite abruptly he asked, What is actually your name?

Peter Pallet. I mumbled, so he couldn't understand the word Pallet.

Why didn't I say: Peter Astrolabe? Only because I was ashamed of the name?

Why did I lie when he asked me about my parents and my home town?

And how old are you?

I lied again, Nineteen. I come from a little town on the coast.

Is all that true?

Yes, I said defiantly. And my parents are dead.

Was your grandfather's name Berengar?

I was so surprised that I fell into his trap.

Yes, that was his name.

And you come from Pallet?

No, I lied out of pure obstinacy.

You can go. You have passed the exam. By the way, don't think too much, it's dangerous; when thinking one can go beyond one's reason, and then one falls into emptiness. Go now, go.

A puzzling speech. The whole scene was puzzling.

It frightened me. Why this sort of interrogation? How did he know the name Berengar? If he knew that, he knew a lot more about me. And had Abelard's resemblance to my grandfather Berengar not struck me from the beginning? Was there a secret there?

I turned around. Abelard was still sitting where I'd left him. But he held his face hidden in his hands. He didn't hear me. I stood still. Was he perhaps crying?

Suddenly he raised his face. He hadn't been crying.

Go, he said, but he said it gently, and then he said, Don't brood, be patient, some day you will understand.

I had no patience. This Abelard: who was he to me? A relative, probably distantly related through my grandfather. But why didn't he tell me that outright?

The curtain was still closed. My parents lived in Pallet; they weren't dead. Why not ride there?

[40]

My alleged mother's puzzling words: Don't believe everything you hear in Paris.

What shouldn't I believe? The matter worried me.

Abelard's lectures were over for that year. I didn't see him anymore.

A few weeks' vacation. I could have ridden to Pallet. I didn't do it. I went on long rides with my friend Roger, a fellow student who also studied with Abelard. A cheerful companion. One evening he told me he had decided to become a monk.

What a notion! Roger, a monk?

Why not.

But you wanted a professorship.

Both are possible. As with Abelard.

Abelard – a monk?

Didn't you know that? He entered monastic life late, in Saint-Denis.

Late. Why?

I don't know exactly, but it was about seventeen or eighteen years ago.

No alarm signal? Nothing. I only asked: Why isn't he in Saint-Denis anymore?

There is no school there anymore, and in any case he had a falling out with the people there.

Why?

Because he pulled the carpet out from under their feet. Because he revealed that the bones they revered as relics were certainly not those of their founder Dionysius the Areopagite. But they didn't want to admit it. How would they look if it got out that the bones they worshipped were not those of their founder, that indeed there was no such Greek bishop. They would also lose their source of income, because the monastery lived on the money of devout pilgrims. Well, and then Abelard had to leave the monastery. They made him the abbot in a Godforsaken spot in Brittany, in Saint-Gildas, until he was allowed to come back to Paris again.

I felt a rope around my neck; it was still loose, but I felt it. Saint-Gildas? And Dionysius the Areopagite, about whom Abelard had asked me and of whom

I knew nothing, although according to Abelard I was one of his followers. How was that connected?

Roger, what do you know about Abelard?

Only what everyone knows.

And what does everyone know?

What I told you.

Nothing else?

You'll have to ask others, for example the canon Fulbert.

Not him, no.

What do you have against him?

He's a malicious dwarf.

Then perhaps Master John. Or the physician Anselm. He's the same age as Abelard – I suppose they studied together – and he's also the son of a knight from the north.

Like Abelard?

Like Abelard.

What else do you know? Spit it out!

There's nothing to spit out. I really know nothing more.

So now the journey to the medic Anselm. But what and how should I ask him?

Three times I turned around, three times I came back.

He must have heard my steps because he opened the door and said, Come in. What seems to be the matter?

I'm not ill, I said recalcitrantly.

Then why have you come to a physician?

At that moment my visit, which was a surprise visit, seemed quite senseless to me. Excuse me, I said, and wanted to leave.

Do sit down, you're pale and out of breath, rest a little, drink a little wine.

The wine and the physician's voice loosened the knots in my neck and loosened my tongue.

I'm not ill, but . . .

What is tormenting you? What do you fear? An exam?

I just passed one, with Master Abelard.

Are you suffering because of a woman?

No, certainly not. I only want to find out something about Master Abelard.

What? He is a public figure and your teacher. What else is there to know?

At that moment I knew my question; it came to me in a flash: Was he always a monk?

No. But no man has always been a monk, one becomes one.

Yes, of course. But what was Master Abelard before he became a monk?

A teacher at various universities.

And otherwise, how was he? You knew him, didn't you, when he was young.

Very bright and recalcitrant.

I peeled the onion and peeled the onion and didn't get to the truth. Now fate helped me: the physician's question about my name. He dragged it out of me.

Peter Astrolabe.

He took a few steps backward and repeated, Astrolabe. Astrolabe. Astrolabe. Then he asked my age, or rather he said, You're eighteen, aren't you?

How do you know that? Do you know me?

His hesitation. His strange look. His question about my parents' names.

I don't know. They are dead. I am an orphan.

What a lie. Did I turn red or, perhaps, pale?

Your grandfather's name is Berengar.

That wasn't a question. He didn't ask; he knew.

What else?

You know your father.

A pause. The quiet before a storm, before the first clap of thunder. I waited as if paralyzed.

Come here, said the physician.

He took a piece of paper and wrote on it ABELARD. And underneath my name: ASTROLABE.

ABELARD

ADRLABE

↓ ↓

ASTROLABE

Do you understand? It's an anagram. The letters are interchanged.

At that moment I fainted for the first time in my life.

The physician held my hand. When I came to, he said, You had to find out sometime.

I pulled myself together. If I have a father, then I also have a mother. Who is she? Is her name Denise?

Her name is Heloise.

Is she alive?

She is alive.

And where?

She's a nun.

My father a monk, my mother a nun.

I laughed in horror.

No, it's not like that. Your father wasn't a monk when he fathered you, and your mother wasn't a nun. You are a legitimate child. You are the child of a great love, a tragic love.

Tragic. Abelard's exam question: Is one free to choose between good and evil?

But was evil involved? What was the choice? Tragic. If it was that, then fate had set a trap into which those two had to fall, inevitably. But how does it stand with me, called into life in tragic love? Was that tragic love a forbidden love?

I was close to the truth and yet far away from it.

Then Fulbert's word occurred to me: Abelard, that whoremonger.

I had forgotten it. But now it was there.

Whoremonger.

I forced myself to ask.

That, said the physician, is slander. Abelard was never what is meant by that. Who said it?

The canon Fulbert.

That spiteful tongue. Abelard never visited a whore and never had affairs with women. He lived austerely. He knew nothing but his work.

But I? A legitimate child? Is that true?

Yes and no. You were fathered before the marriage. The marriage itself was a secret one.

So there is a stigma.

That is for God to decide. I see only fate. It was too difficult for two people. But let me tell you, they were both noble enough to take responsibility for it. But the stakes were high in this game.

And I? Why did I know nothing of my parents? If they were married and I was legitimate, then why this secret?

A forced secret.

A forced marriage.

Forced, yes, but differently from what you think.

At that time a girl called Heloise lived in Paris. This sentence – like the beginning of a fairy tale. Once upon a time. Yes, and at that time a man called Abelard lived in Paris.

What I found out that day wasn't the whole story, but I did find out the most important parts, and all the rest was added gradually. Once on the right track, I found all the rest.

The story began with Fulbert. He had a niece, or only a ward, Heloise. She lived with him. All his ambition was for her.

When I speak the name Fulbert, I feel like throwing up. A revolting, toothless, drooling old man who hated Abelard.

Justifiably, from his point of view. But wasn't it simply that he received the punishment his ambition provoked? He loved Heloise in his own way, that is, he was proud of her, he saw her as his creature. And she met his expectations. She was clever by nature, she learned easily, she learned Greek and Hebrew, she read classical literature and was already known among scholars when she was seventeen years old. She was truly exceptional. Fulbert wanted her star to rise even higher.

At that time there lived in Paris a man by the name of Abelard, forty years old and famous. Fulbert chose him and no less a person than him as the teacher for his Heloise. He came into the house daily as the teacher and gave Heloise private lessons. For that, Fulbert had to pay a fee. Abelard's friends persuaded him that it was cheaper to have the teacher move right in. They already knew of the love affair and of Abelard's wish to be together with Heloise day and night. And Fulbert was miserly. Instead of his paying a fee, Abelard had to pay him for room and board. A simple calculation.

Abelard describes it in detail in his *Life Confession*:

Fulbert arrived at the goal of his wishes: Abelard's money for himself, and his learning for his niece. And I too arrived at the goal of my wishes: Fulbert begged me for more than I had dared hope for in my boldest dreams, and he himself provided the opportunity for my love. He left Heloise's advanced education totally up to me. I could teach her whenever my lectures left me time to do so, during the day or the night, and if I had the impression that she was lazy, I was to beat her mercilessly. This type and this extent of naivety did surprise me considerably. I couldn't have been more astonished if he had given his delicate lamb into the protection of a ravenously hungry wolf.

The ravenously hungry wolf and the delicate lamb. I'm laughing out loud. A lamb, a delicate one: the wrong image. The delicate lamb had the power of a tigress. That would become evident.

But what the hell was Fulbert thinking when he brought Abelard, a handsome man in his prime, into the house? Could Fulbert really think that would work out well?

He could believe it, precisely because Abelard was no whoremonger but, rather, puritanical, at least to all appearances, and tremendously ambitious; he wouldn't risk his meteoric career for a love affair. He was a canon, and that meant not only that he wouldn't marry, but also that he would have an irreproachable reputation. At any rate, if there was something reproachable, it wasn't allowed to come to light. Abelard was irreproachable. Almost incredible, when one knows the frenzied love of which he was capable.

And Heloise? Did Fulbert consider her a child who needed beating when she was lazy? Hadn't he noticed she had grown into a woman? Did he think she consisted solely of reason and academic ambition? Or did he think that the difference in age would keep the two apart? Mustn't he have known that it is customary for a knight to marry late and to take a much younger wife? He was forty; she was seventeen. Could so young a girl love a man who was so much older? Or was Fulbert unable to imagine that a woman would love this confirmed bachelor Abelard and, even less, that he would be able to love? But what did the withered little man Fulbert know of love?

The trap of fate snapped shut. "The shared house was soon followed by shared hearts." And the shared hearts were followed by what had to follow. Abelard describes it with great pleasure in his *Life Confession*. Did he regret it? I read words of remorse, but I don't believe them. By ruthlessly accusing himself, he, the eloquent dialectician, simultaneously manages to praise and exalt himself, so that one excuses his shadows for the sake of his illuminating greatness. There is exaggeration in his self-accusation. He always exaggerated. He even exaggerates when he speaks of the time of his great love affair with Heloise.

You know what shameless things we got involved in through my unbridled lust. I wallowed almost like an animal in that mire, even during Holy Week and on the highest feast days. Often I even went so far as to use threats and blows to make you submit to my wishes when you offered resistance and when you, the weak woman, begged me to do without for once. The heat of my lust had almost forged me together with you. I no longer thought of God or of my better self, so deeply had I immersed myself in the miserable delights that are too filthy for me even to name without blushing.

Thus Abelard.

What the hell did these two do together? "Shameless things." What? My imagination is working. I'm afraid of the images that come to mind. I'm afraid of seeing my parents have sexual intercourse. My mother in the arms of that wild man with the cruel face. He wrote that he forced her to have intercourse when she didn't want to. He hit her! He hit her. . . . The right to punish her that had been expressly given to him by Fulbert. He hit her until she complied with his wishes. And she put up with it? Of course, of course. After all, she felt that he loved her. Perhaps it was a subtle pleasure for both of them to hit and be hit. "Rather a peculiar sort of caress that gave her more pleasure than pain." Well. To me it is repulsive. Try to understand me, Mother.

When Fulbert finally found out about the love affair, he threw Abelard out of the house. Too late, too late. As if he could really have separated the two.

By doing so, he forged our hearts together more than ever; our love, frustrated as it now was, flared up all the more strongly. In the eyes of the world, we were now dishonored once and for all. Therefore, we no longer needed to show the world any consideration. That we owed this loss of honor to our carnal desires seemed to us a priceless asset. So in us was repeated what Ovid told about Mars and Venus and the troubled fortune of their love.

The two were envied by one person, the sinister blacksmith Hephaestus. He loved the beautiful Venus with unrequited love. He couldn't separate the pair, but he could betray them and expose them to the laughter of the gods. He captured them like rabbits: He forged a net and threw it over the two of them so they could be seen by all in the middle of their loveplay.

And then? I asked the physician.

The physician said, You were already there at that time, a tiny embryo. Without the blessing of the church, with Fulbert's curse.

And Heloise?

She was ecstatic.

And Abelard?

He eloped with her without hesitation and brought her to Pallet, where you were born and grew up as the son of your aunt Denise.

And what else?

Fulbert was furious. Abelard returned to Paris and had to fear Fulbert's revenge. But he was no coward; he was a knight. So he went straight to Fulbert, asked his forgiveness, and offered to do anything to make amends. He even appealed to Fulbert's understanding for human weakness and the strength of love. As if the dried-out little man Fulbert could have understanding for that. He who had never loved, neither man nor woman. This allusion to the power of Eros was exactly the wrong thing, because what made this little man so poisonous was his envy of Abelard's male potency. This Abelard, who had seduced Heloise in the twinkling of an eye or, rather, who had allowed himself to be seduced by her in the twinkling of an eye, because it certainly was the woman who seduced the man. Fulbert's logic developed cracks at this point. Who had to be punished: surely the seductress, not he who was seduced.

Fulbert hatched out his plan of revenge. He had admired Abelard, perhaps in his barren mind had loved him, but he had also fiercely envied him as a scholar.

At first everything seemed to go well, better than Fulbert could hope for: Abelard spoke of marriage. But a secret marriage. Why secret? Especially when the love affair was known throughout the city. Or didn't people know how far this affair had already gone? Did people take it for a subtle friendship and Abelard's songs for the usual *chansons* of a troubadour to any woman, a nameless one? Hadn't Abelard during that time become a poor teacher who canceled lectures? Hadn't he changed? Couldn't one see that he was having a secret amour? Now the marriage. Secret. Was Heloise of such low origin that Abelard, the nobleman, the knight, would be ashamed to enter into a marriage unbefitting his rank? That was certainly not the case. Since if Heloise had been of the lower nobility, her early fame would nevertheless have elevated her far above her class. Also, Abelard was not the man to be bothered about class differences. They got married. But secretly. That it didn't remain a secret was Fulbert's evil work. At first, though, it did in fact take place in secret.

Why though, why?

Because Abelard was a canon? A canon is no priest, therefore not obliged for better or for worse to celibacy. I too am a canon. If I wanted to marry, I would lose my position, and with it the ground under my feet, in every regard, morally and financially. But Abelard? Wasn't it all the same to him whether he was a canon or not? He was a professor. He had the lecture fees. He was a scholar. But wasn't that the real reason? Would it damage his reputation as an academic if he were married? What was the connection? None. So one might say. But Heloise had something to say in the matter. Something that made a decisive difference. But I found out about that only much later. I found it out in bits and pieces. I only now found out the whole story, Mother, when I read your letters and my father's *Story of My Misfortunes*.

[49]

You are difficult to understand, Mother. What an ambitious woman you were. Ambitious for your lover and in a clever way for yourself – or shall we say for an idea. What inhuman parents I have!

At that time, after my first conversation and a following one with the physician, I was furious with the two of you and with everything: two people loved each other, brought a child into the world, and deserted it; guilt upon guilt. But I put the main blame on the man. After all, he had fathered me. He had to know what he was doing. He, not Heloise, who was after all still a girl. A little lamb, taken by the wolf and left lying half dead.

That was my version of the story at that time.

It was as false as it was true.

It is false that Heloise was really the little lamb that was taken by the wolf and abandoned.

It is true that Abelard didn't want to abandon her and that she herself didn't want the marriage. In any case, what I found out from a friend of the physician's is true. He was a friend of Abelard's and a witness at his wedding.

A sad wedding. Bride and bridegroom were already in the church. They had spent the night there. Praying. The bride's face, so the witness says, showed she had been crying. The bridegroom was pale and stern. He had achieved what he wanted: a legal marriage. The bride looked as if she might faint at any moment, but she made it through the ceremony. Naturally, Fulbert was present.

Later I read in Abelard's *Story of My Misfortunes*: "Each of us also had a few relatives present."

Who may they have been? Did Heloise have any relatives? I never found out who they were.

After the wedding ceremony there was no celebration. Of course not. The two, now a married couple before God and the witnesses, did not go home together. Where indeed would their common home have been? In the pale light of dawn each went a separate way, very quietly and furtively. No one was supposed to find out they were married. It wasn't Abelard who had reasons for that, but Heloise all the more and stronger ones. But at that time I didn't know them.

For me, the account of the witness, together with everything that I now knew or suspected, was cause for a fierce hatred of Abelard and for an equally strong sympathy for my mother.

But where was she?

Abelard had sent her to a convent. But which one? Neither the physician nor his friend knew. So they said. However, I believe they knew and didn't want to tell me. They probably considered me capable of that foolish act that I actually wanted to commit and almost did commit: abduct my mother.

Now I can talk about it with some calm. At that time I was beside myself.

There were several convents in the city and in the vicinity. I rode from one to another, but I didn't dare approach the entrance gate. What should I ask? Who would answer me, who would tell the truth? Perhaps she had changed her name, perhaps she was far away from Paris, perhaps in an isolated place like Saint-Gildas.

I could go to Fulbert. He had to know where she was. Why not simply go to him and say, I am Astrolabe, the son of Heloise. Where is she? Out with it. Did you have her killed?

I imagined the scene. The old man was so frail that he couldn't leap up. He would sit on his chair as if tied to it. Toothless as he was, he could hardly talk, only hiss, and he would have to listen to everything that I spat in his face, and again and again the question: Where is my mother?

But I didn't go to Fulbert. I was too proud to attack that defenseless little man.

Suddenly – why only now? – I remembered the forest with the dilapidated huts and the woodcutter who had shown me from a distance the convent with the unusual name "Paraclete." A nun lives there, a prioress, an exceptional woman. Or how did he say? She was still young and already famous, but too beautiful for the convent, and sometimes a man came on horseback, a monk, a priest who preached there, he had been a famous scholar.

The convent: The Paraclete. And the young prioress: Heloise. And the man who came to preach: Abelard. So that's how it is. The next day I rode to the Paraclete, lost my way, and finally stood in front of a monastery. The gate was open; I walked in and saw monks, no nuns. That wasn't the Paraclete, it was Argenteuil.

The monk at the gate said, This monastery belongs to us, to the Abbey of Saint-Denis. We have old rights here; the nuns had none.

And so you simply threw them out, chased them away like stray dogs?

They had no right to be here.

So that is how you treat your sisters in Christ.

When necessary, yes.

And where did they go?

That I don't know. That is their business, not ours. Some went home, others sought a new convent, somewhere.

Somewhere. For example?

How does it concern you?

I'm looking for a nun, a relative.

Well, just go ahead and look. There are all kinds of small convents around here.

Was there a nun here by the name of Heloise?

Not a clue. Do you think I take note of nuns' names?

She was the prioress.

Oh, her! God knows where she is. And now leave me in peace.

I went.

So that was one of the monks from Saint-Denis. How impolite, how coarse, and all his answers were imbued with hate. Why? What did they have against Heloise here? They had something against Abelard and readily transferred that to Heloise.

Chased away. Where did Heloise go? I imagined Heloise, my mother, wandering through the woods, alone and without protection. But the woodcutter had told me she was in the Paraclete and was even prioress.

I seemed to be jinxed: I didn't find the convent.

I remembered that dense forest with the dilapidated wooden huts, but the huts had disappeared and I didn't encounter anyone. Fate was against me and my plan to abduct my mother. The longer I wandered about, the wilder my plans became. But night fell, without moon and stars, and I was afraid of getting totally lost. So I returned to the city.

A sleepless night. The abduction plan seemed increasingly untenable to me. Why should I abduct her? Perhaps she didn't even want to be free. And how should I abduct her, even if she were in agreement?

By daybreak the plan had vanished.

But as if the devil had a hand in it, it was, as it were, forced on me again. An ill wind blew on the embers.

I encountered the physician in a narrow street. Whoever one meets there cannot be avoided. But why should I avoid him? Or why he me?

At that moment it occurred to me that he had to know whether my mother was really in the Paraclete. Or it could be altogether different. I got right to the point.

Please tell me where I can find my mother.

He looked at me with concern. Dear Peter, he said. He said it in a tone that put me off, it sounded like a warning. What did he know of my thoughts and plans that I kept secret even from myself?

He repeated, Dear Peter. And after a pause, Leave your mother where she is, leave her in her peace that she attained with such difficulty, don't touch the old wound.

Wound? I asked and was already on the lookout.

Come, he said, come into my house with me; this is no conversation for the street; you know the Parisian ears, all of Paris is one single ear for catching every bit of gossip.

Hasn't the gossip about my parents long since subsided? Doesn't it bore the Parisians? They are always bent on the latest rumor.

If there doesn't happen to be a new one, an old one is dragged out and dressed up again. Come along.

The conversation with the physician was oil on the fire and wind on the flame. I remained completely calm. I was able to deceive him. He considered me mature enough to hear the story.

Well, Peter, your mother as you know entered a convent and went first of all to Argenteuil. She had been there as a young girl in boarding school, and so it seemed natural that she went there again after everything that happened. You've already found out what happened to Abelard, your father. Fulbert's abominable revenge.

Yes, I know. Poor, stupid Fulbert. He envied Abelard everything: his fame, the students' love, his mind, all in all his fascination. He probably thought he could destroy that fascination by the castration. As if Abelard's fascination emanated from his testicles.

I spoke very calmly. I was waiting like the cat before the mouse hole. I wanted to hear something about my mother, the nun. But what? Was there yet another secret?

There was one, a grave one, the gravest; the one that Heloise could not get over all her life. I read it only lately in her letters. The physician didn't say or didn't know everything. What he did know was that Abelard and Heloise were officially married, but it was kept secret. Fulbert, the poisonous snake, betrayed the secret. He was obsessed with hatred over the betrayal that Heloise, the so dearly loved girl, and Abelard, the highly esteemed, had perpetrated on him in his house. They had courted right in front of him and he hadn't noticed. That had made him a laughingstock, a cuckold, as it were, and he could not get over it. Although Abelard wanted and carried out the marriage with Heloise, his anger was not abated. On the contrary. Heloise knew her uncle; she feared his revenge. Rightly so. Abelard had brought Heloise to a safe place, to Argenteuil. And so that she would be completely safe, she was taken in and clothed as a lay sister. So she was out of the game. He remained. And he was castrated. The unforgettable morning when it all happened. Half the city crowded in front of Abelard's house. The students were beside themselves. As were the clerics. And many Parisian citizens. One could see from their pain and anger how loved and respected Abelard was. He was in despair. I was with him, I attended to his wound. He was in terrible pain. But it was nothing in comparison to the pain of his soul. The disgrace, the disgrace. A eunuch. People will point at me and laugh at me. The laughingstock of all Paris. The malicious joy of my enemies. I can never show myself in public again. I have fallen from my height. My fame is gone. My career ended. And the word of God that the emasculated are an abomination before him and that castrated animals may not be used as sacrificial animals. In Deuteronomy it says no eunuch can enter into the assembly of the Lord.

So he complained and raged. I calmed him, The laws of the Old Testament no longer apply to us. But it also says in the New Testament, he cried, in the New: A eunuch cannot become a priest.

I asked the physician if it was important to Abelard to become a priest.

So it seems. Incidentally, it didn't prevent him from becoming one later on. In any case, he came as a priest to the Paraclete to celebrate mass there.

Well, now, I said, so everything straightened itself out for him. Yes, for him. And Heloise? While Abelard was complaining, he didn't say a word about Heloise, did he? You must know, you were there and heard everything.

He didn't speak of her.

Strange. Yet she had been his wife and been sharing his bed.

Had been. Now she is a nun.

How so? She had simply been brought to a safe place. But that doesn't mean that she had to become a nun.

But she did.

I understand: there was no other option for her. Her husband castrated and ostracized and no longer a professor, a nobody, what was he still to her?

Peter, how you talk. Shame on you. You have no idea what your mother is like. Do you think she would have abandoned him in his hour of need?

If she loved him, she would have left the convent to live with him. They could have gone to Pallet or to other relatives.

In that, you know your father even less than your mother: he didn't just want to survive anywhere, he didn't want to leave Paris, he had to find some kind of work that suited his genius.

He found it.

Yes, he found it. He found it very soon, but not for long, fortunately for him. He fled, as it were, under cover of darkness to Saint-Denis. He hid. The hiding place did not remain a secret. The physical wound was hardly healed when clerics and students came and besought him to teach again. The abbot of Saint-Denis didn't hold him back. On the contrary, he was glad to be rid of this critical thinker, this all too keen observer. You see, the monastery had fallen into disrepute because of its lack of discipline. In any case, Abelard found many serious irregularities there and said what he thought. At first to the abbot alone, then in the monastery in front of all the monks. Once again, he made many enemies. And so it was fine with everyone when he went.

Where?

To a hermitage.

To the Paraclete?

That's what he called the settlement later.

I was there once, without knowing what had happened.

You don't know that? This hermitage competed with the Paris university. Many students ran after their teacher Abelard. He was, in spite of everything, the great Abelard. Actually it was a sort of monastic community: all lived in poverty, and Abelard lived from what his students brought him.

So it was a happy time. Until the envy, the hatred of his enemies tracked him down. I know. The two from Reims, who simply took him away like a criminal.

How do you know that?

A woodcutter told me. But my question remains unanswered: Where is my mother?

I told you, didn't I? She is a nun in the Convent of the Paraclete.

Abelard had hidden her there. Fine. But she didn't have to stay. Why did she stay? Why then, why still today?

Where else should she go? Maybe she was glad to be there.

Yes, who knows. Since she couldn't be or rather didn't want to be Abelard's wife, she could be a nun and make a career for herself in the order: soon she was the prioress, and that was no low position. And since she wasn't allowed to have a son, she could have and guide daughters. So everything was fine. Or was it?

No, it wasn't fine, not at all. How could it turn out well when you, Mother, didn't voluntarily become a nun. He was the one who wanted it. And you obeyed. That, however, was not as it was in the Jephthah story. It wasn't even like that with Abraham and Isaac. When God ordered Abraham to offer up his son, Isaac, it was only a test, a trial. This strange Old Testament God

[56]

loved sacrifices. Animal sacrifices. Human sacrifices. A violent Lord. An angry Lord, who demanded inhuman behavior of his loyal follower Abraham: he should offer up his son, his only son, the late-born son, the most precious and beloved of Abraham's possessions. Go, take firewood, go to such-and-such a place, erect an altar of stones, and then sacrifice your son to me. Abraham obeyed. His son carried the wood that was to be used to burn him. They came to a place that appealed to God. Here then. And Abraham erected the stone altar. Naturally Isaac asked, And where is the sacrificial animal? His father said, The Most High will take care of that. He had already taken care of that. The sacrificial animal was already present. So Abraham bound his son as if he were a lamb and laid him on the stone altar. And what did the son say? Wasn't he surprised? Didn't he resist? Didn't he scream? Didn't he try to flee? No. He lay still. He saw his father draw the knife. Everything seemed decided, terribly finally decided. Then at the last moment the Highest One intervened and restrained Abraham. Stop. Enough. I see you are a God-fearing man. Untie your son. There is another sacrificial animal: a ram is caught there in the undergrowth. So it's the ram instead of the son.

I ask myself how the son reacted to the matter. Mustn't he have feared and secretly hated his father? And mustn't he have hated this cruel tester God?

Did Heloise hate the priest who sacrificed her? She loved him. She loved him beyond all measure. Isaac did not know who was supposed to be the sacrificial animal. He was full of innocence and trust. But Heloise: she knew that there was no other sacrificial animal but she. And she went. And no angel of the Lord came to prevent that sacrifice. The lamb laid itself on the altar. Really? Did you really voluntarily become a nun, Mother Heloise?

Doesn't one become a monk or nun when one is expressly called to it by God? You weren't called, Mother! And you knew it. And yet you went.

Why, why? Because Abelard wanted it that way. So you were forced? No, not that either. Did he order you to do it? No. Did Abelard's God order him to sacrifice you? His God? His God was his ambition. I want to be fair: ambition and despairing love. In any case: self-interest. Monstrous, rapacious, blasphemous self-interest. What did he write in his *Story of My Misfortunes*? "At my insistence, and before I took my vows, Heloise had already submitted to my will and become a nun." So that is how my mother voluntarily entered the convent. But must Abelard not have known that a forced vow is not binding? It is invalid, it is sinful. But was it forced? What subtle differences. Did Abelard have a right at all to tell his wife what to do with her life? But what is a right? Could he order her to take the veil? He could do more than that: he could blackmail her. What is it if not blackmail when a man wishes of his beloved wife that she enter a convent in order to prove her love and loyalty to him? Didn't she say she loved him above all else and wanted to share his fate and remain true to him until death? She said it and meant it seriously. Deadly seriously. Didn't she write to him: "Even now I know only one thing, only your will"? And she continues: "It wasn't pious submission to God's will that led me, a young girl, into the dark convent; no, your will alone drove me to enter the convent." That is a hard, clear, sharp word: "drove me to enter the convent." Was it really like that? Did he drive you, Mother? Didn't you go voluntarily because he wanted you to? Is that a contradiction? Jephthah's daughter voluntarily let herself be sacrificed, or wasn't it voluntarily? Wasn't she bound by the promise that her father had given to his God? Voluntarily bound. And Isaac? Couldn't he flee from his father? Surely he was a strong boy: why did he let himself be bound like a lamb? Why did his father actually bind him? Was this father counting on the sacrificial animal being able to flee? But the sacrificial animal let himself be bound. Again the dialectic: voluntarily bound. Heloise let herself be bound. But not without complaining. The lamb screamed. It screamed all its life. I have read your letters, Mother. But only recently.

After my conversation with the physician, I was again tormented by the plan of abducting my mother from her convent prison. But did she want to be abducted? I had to know that first. Who could tell me but she herself? And would she tell me? Who was I to her? Would she recognize me as her son? Would she confide in me? Would she want to go with me? No, she wouldn't want to flee. A woman like her does not flee. And why flee? She could simply leave the convent and go somewhere. Or couldn't she? The nun's vow. Did that bind her for her entire life? A forced vow . . . My thoughts were running in a circle. Another sleepless night. Morning found me, apparently, reasonable. My plan: First I had to know with all certainty whether my mother was in the Convent of the Paraclete. After all, she could have been brought to another convent. Therefore, a ride to the Paraclete.

The forest! How familiar it was. The huts of course had disappeared, the dense undergrowth was thinned out, and a road, good for riding, led to the convent. How orderly it all was. The convent still quite new. Young plantations all around. Someone ruled here who made sure that order prevailed. A woman. The prioress. Or abbess. So she was here.

Two young women were working in the plantation. Not nuns. I spoke to them.

Parisians from the suburbs. From Argenteuil. Why were they here, not there? Because the nuns had been driven away from there.

Why?

Because Argenteuil belongs to the monastery at Saint-Denis.

If that is true, said the other. The abbot there simply asserted that.

And did no one protest? (I thought of Abelard.)

What good would that have done? The abbot was a friend of the king.

And the nuns?

At first they all ran away, anywhere. Like a flock of frightened hens.

And wasn't a prioress by the name of Heloise there?

Yes, but she was powerless. But then the convent here was given to her.

Given by whom?

By the one who had it built, Abelard.

Who is that? I asked slyly.

Who is he? You don't know? But he's famous everywhere, a professor. To be sure, he had many enemies, among them the abbot of Saint-Denis. And that's the reason the nuns were driven out. He had nothing against the nuns, but he had something against Abelard.

What?

That I don't know.

But why did he drive out the nuns?

One beats the donkey and means the farmer.

So that's how it is. But I still don't understand what Abelard and the nuns have to do with each other.

Well, something happened to one of them.

What?

The other woman, who had been silent until then, said, Shut up.

And to me she said, What business is it of yours, young man?

She was rude. That provoked me, and as often happened, I don't know what got into me. I couldn't be silent.

What business is it of mine? It concerns me what happened to that woman before she entered the convent. I am what happened to her. I happened to her.

She didn't understand, and it was best that way. I had said it in my Breton dialect. I left the two standing there, tethered my horse, and went up to the gate. Happened, happened, like an accident happens to someone. The two had certainly not understood my obscenity. They couldn't guess who had spoken with them there. But if these two women knew something of my mother's fate . . . But what was it they knew? Happened, happened, something that drove her to enter the convent. Some man who drove her to enter it. The gate that was shut forever.

I approached the gate quickly and resolutely. The matter seemed quite simple: I would ask to see the prioress Heloise to discuss something with her.

I knocked with the wooden mallet. Behind the double wooden bars a shadow appeared, who asked me what I wanted.

I would like to visit the prioress.

She isn't receiving anyone now.

When will she be?

What do you wish of her?

That concerns only her and me.

We are a convent, and everything concerns everyone here.

I'm not sure that is also the opinion of your prioress. Please tell her that a young man from Pallet is here, a student, a relative, a very close relative.

Your name?

Should I say it? No. That was dangerous. That could ruin my entire plan.

Tell her: a nephew of Denise from Pallet. That will suffice.

[60]

A rustling of wide skirts, a trailing sound on the flagstone floor, a scurrying of sandals. The closing of the door inaudible. "That will suffice," I had said. For what? That Heloise didn't want to see me?

I already feared I had said too much. Futile. Pointless.

My horse whinnied again and pawed the ground. So run for it. Just get out of here.

Then the door opened, and again the rustling and trailing of skirts. Damned darkness in this room where people turned into shadows. But there: the voice. Quiet, but firm:

Why do you come? What will you gain if you see your mother? She has suffered enough. Grant her her difficult peace. Go! Live your life. Yours, do you hear? And after a while, already from the door, Go, Astrolabe! Farewell! Adieu!

Were there tears in her voice?

The door clicked shut.

That had been her, Heloise, my mother.

I beat on the wooden bars, I screamed, Mother!

She had to hear the scream. The whole convent must have heard it.

No answer came. Never, never again.

There was no sense in waiting. I gave up.

I screamed, Fine, if you want it that way! and ran out.

I forgot my horse. I ran aimlessly, crying with utter rage, and I screamed, Abelard, you lecher, seducer of my mother, whoremonger, you deserved to be castrated, I hate you, I'll kill you, I have to kill you to avenge my mother. You dishonored her. That must be punished by death. And I will be your legitimate murderer. Judge and executioner. Am I not from a long line of knights? Isn't it my duty to avenge our family? I will free you from your captivity, Mother, I, your son. I!

I ran back to the convent. How could I abduct her? Not through the gate. How else? The wall was high and wide. Was there a place that could be breached? If I broke out stones day by day? But how would I bring the prioress to this place? So another way: bribe a gang of soldiers or, for all I cared, robbers to storm the convent. But I had too little money. How about my fellow students? Would they be prepared to help me? They would have to be enemies of Abelard. Perhaps the monks of Saint-Gildas? Too far away.

Simpler and more effective: throw firebrands into the convent so that the nuns would have to flee, and I would grab my mother, on my horse with her and away. Where to? Away, away. To Pallet. But if she didn't want to be freed? If she wanted, wouldn't she long since have been able to go? What held her behind those dark walls? Her vow? The duty to her husband? No, no, nothing held her but her tremendously obstinate love. Abelard's slave! I cried. No one but he has power over you, Mother! If I succeeded in abducting you: where would you want to flee? To him, where else. And he would bring you here again, because you would want it so. And I, what would I have gained? A mother? No. She wouldn't love me; she would never forgive me. I would have gambled everything away.

So that's out.

If I could speak with her. Should I try it one more time? Not right away. No hasty moves.

What would be possible, though: to kill Abelard.

If I had known then what I later found out from your letters, Mother, I would have killed him. Truly. I swear to you.

What I didn't know then: Abelard not only demanded that Heloise become a nun, but also that she do so before he himself entered Saint-Denis as a monk. In fact, it was this for which she reproached him with sharp bitterness. Only this, but this vehemently enough and often enough. Today I know exactly what happened then: Abelard, castrated and apparently expelled from the clerical and academic world, felt destroyed. He was ashamed of his condition. Like a sick animal, he felt the urge to creep into hiding. He hid in the monastery at Saint-Denis. He decided to become a monk. That was his business. But was it his business to demand of Heloise that she too enter a convent? Didn't I read in your letter:

It wasn't pious submission to God's will that led me as a young girl into the dark convent; no, your will alone drove me to enter the convent. If I get no thanks from you for my sacrifice, then even you must consider it in vain, because I can expect no reward from God, because I didn't do what I did out of love for God.

But why did he drive her to enter the convent? Because he himself became a monk. One becomes a monk in order to sacrifice oneself to God. Abelard's lie: He didn't sacrifice himself, he hid himself. But did he sacrifice Heloise? Why? Or did his sacrifice consist of doing without her? Did he do without her? Not at all. On the contrary, he bound his beloved all the more firmly to himself. Now that she, being a nun, could belong to no other, she belonged entirely to him. To him, Abelard, not to God. He didn't need to fear that she loved God more than him. She didn't love God. If she even spoke to this God, then in bitter accusation. He was to blame for the suffering in her life. He. And Abelard.

She let herself be driven to enter the convent. Voluntarily. No, not that. But her absolute love of Abelard was voluntary. Other women sacrifice themselves to God. Heloise's God was Abelard. He could demand what only God could demand: the sacrifice of her life. God could require the unheard-of from Abraham and Isaac. But Abelard wasn't God. He was simply an extremely jealous man, and a demoniacally egoistic one: If he was robbed of his masculinity, then she should be robbed of her femininity. Because he could no longer lie with a woman, she should no longer be allowed to lie with a man. That was the logic of it.

For Abelard. Not for Heloise. There remained something irreconcilable.

I want to tell you frankly: It hurt me bitterly that I found so little trust in you. God knows, at your command I would unhesitatingly have hurried on ahead of you or plunged after you into hell.

Voluntarily. But not forced in such a disgusting fashion. He demanded of her not only that which she finally granted him with the voluntariness of boundless love: the entry into the convent. Oh no, that wasn't enough for him. Not reliable enough: she had to enter before him. Before him.

He was so unsure of her. He even writes that frankly to her:

It could have happened that I withdrew from the world but you didn't find the way that led out of the world, be it from listening to your relatives or to the temptations of the flesh.

Quite simply, therefore: he didn't trust your love and loyalty, and you knew that, and that was what caused you extreme suffering. He didn't know you. He didn't know the magnitude and purity of your love. He considered it possible that you could love another. He was so uncertain of you that he insisted that you had to take the vow before he did. Only when he knew that you were behind bars, behind cloister bars and thick walls, chained to the monastic vow, only then was he sure of you.

The worst injury he could inflict on your feelings.

Abelard lies when he writes, "So the two of us put on the holy robe together, I in the Abbey of Saint-Denis, Heloise in the Convent of Saint-Argenteuil."

That would be beautiful: both together, on the same day, at the same hour, admittedly separated spatially, but most intimately united; a second marriage, "until death do us part." But that's not how it was. Abelard wasn't yet a monk when you became a nun. Couldn't you with the same right doubt his loyalty? Could he, still a handsome man, a sensual man (you know him), take another lover? Despite his mutilation he remained a man of passion. Couldn't you think, Once I am behind bars and he can no longer satisfy his sensual urges with me, why shouldn't he do so somewhere else? But you weren't capable of such a thought, of such a miserable calculation. You trusted him blindly. But you suffered terribly. You have never forgotten and forgiven him that. I read it in your letters.

He, however: in order to be quite certain that you were locked up in the convent, he was present when you took the veil. He himself writes:

I cannot forget it; many felt sorry for this youthful child and pointed out warningly to her that she would have to find monastic life in all its gravity an unbearable pain. In vain. Crying and sobbing, she called out Cornelia's plaintive words from Lucanus's epos *Pharsalia*:

O glorious husband,
Worthy of a better marriage bed!
Why did fate have to strike
A man like you
So hard? Alas, did I have to
Marry you
So that I would become your unlucky star? But now
Receive my sacrifice,
Joyously I bring it to you.

That was her farewell to the world. With a determined step she went up to the altar, quickly took the veil consecrated by the bishop from the altar, and took her vow before the assembled congregation.

Thus writes Abelard. And in the next sentence he speaks again of himself and his work: Even as a monk the students want him again as their teacher.

And Heloise? But it was only her presence, her youthfulness, her cleverness, her charm that seduced him. How she humbled herself and attributed the blame to herself! And the strange wording of her profession: "Receive my sacrifice." Who should the receiver be? For a nun, God of course. For Heloise it wasn't God. She knew only one god: Abelard. She writes to Abelard about that day:

I hardly dare say it, my love turned into madness; in hopeless despair it sacrificed the only object of its longing. Without hesitation – you, you gave the order – I sacrificed my old robe and my heart, in order to show all the world how I am yours with body and soul. God is my witness, I have always sought only you in you, the quintessential you, not what belongs to you, not your possessions. A firm wedding ring, a gift from you after our wedding night – did I ever ask for those? You are my witness: Not my desire, not my will was my goal, no, only your complete gratification.

Poor Heloise: was he worth it, this man Abelard, that you sacrificed yourself to him?

The shabbiness of his mistrust in your loyalty, Mother, the predatory possessiveness, the brutal egoism! He watched as the lamb was sacrificed. Others wept. And he?

But if someone had told you he wasn't worth the sacrifice of your life, you would have smiled at this ignorance of the greatness of him to whom you brought the sacrifice. How could anyone not see Abelard's greatness, not feel it?

Blind lover, Mother! How could you write him a letter like this one.

What other women believed they had in their husband, I didn't need to believe of you; I knew the truth of my possession and the whole world knew it with me. The genuine depth of my love for you was based on the absence of error. No king, no wise man of this world could have competed with your fame. In all the lands they longed to see you. All women, married or not, were consumed with passionate desire. Every queen envied me the joy of my life and the happiness of my love. . . . Two gifts were given you before others: You were a poet and a singer like no other wise man in this world. When you tired of your philosophical work, you rested on this playground. Your many love songs in classical and modern form live on today. . . . I know of no adornment of the mind or the body in which your youth was not resplendent. . . .

No, no, Mother: Love shouldn't make anyone so blind, so uncritical, so crazy. Didn't you see his shortcomings, shortcomings that everyone saw: his cantankerousness, his megalomania, his vanity, his ingratitude, his diabolical arrogance? Was it your inexperienced youth that made you worship your very first lover without comparison? Or did losing him transfigure your image of him?

And yet: didn't you suddenly have a doubt, Mother?

There is a letter from you to Abelard in which you complain bitterly about the fact that he no longer looks after her, the nun and prioress.

Answer me just one question, if you have an answer: After we had both solemnly taken our vows – I only did so because I was at your disposal – why did I then become so unworthy of you, how could you forget me so completely that I am not allowed to find solace in a letter by your hand? Answer me, if you have an answer, or *I* must

[66]

speak, speak of my suspicion, of all the world's suspicion! What drove you to me was more likely passion rather than friendship, more likely sensual lust than genuine love. And now the passion is dead, and dead all else that had to pave the way for your passion to reach its goal. Oh, if only reproaches would occur to me with which I could excuse you and in some way cover my weakness.

Heloise, Mother: Do you really believe that?

I attribute many bad things to Abelard, but not blind lust. No, he loved you. Not above all else, not that, because above all else he loved his academic work and himself. But he loved you as well as he could love. Perhaps a man cannot love as a woman loves. I don't know because I have never loved and have also never been loved by a woman. I ask myself if I am capable of love at all or even passion. In my dreams, yes, there I lie in wait for girls in dark alleys that have no exits; there I turn into a wolf, pounce on women from behind, dig my claws into their shoulders and breasts, tear their clothes from their bodies, and then I wake up and feel my semen moist on my body. It is quite possible that I, if I found the right woman, would act exactly as Abelard did: mad with pent-up sensuality, I would forget love. But Abelard, no, he loved. First he desired the young body, then he found the mind and the soul, and loved. Or was it the other way around? But was the desire killed by the castration? The physician, whom I asked in my ignorance, said: No, the desire remains, just the organ for giving full expression to it is missing. I ask myself if it doesn't then burn all the more intensely or smoulder like the glowing wood in a charcoal pile. But what concern is that of mine?

The letter in which Heloise writes bitterly of her and Abelard's past love relationship remains strange. How could you, Mother, suddenly think so lowly of him whom you loved so much? Aren't you ashamed of believing evil gossip? Don't you understand that it is envy that whispers in your ear? No, Mother, no: he loved you. Hadn't he led an ascetic life before he saw you? You woke him up, and that was your fate.

And, dear Mother, may your son tell you, the girl Heloise, something? Admittedly he has only theoretical experience, but he is very sure of this: There is no love without sensual desire. You were people, hotblooded, and

[67]

not sexless angels. Would you really have wanted just one of those pale, noble, holy friendships that the two of you read into the writings of Seneca and Theophrastus and other classical pagan philosophers? You took as gospel what was really only the self-interested reflections of men who gave out as holy virtue their Manichaean heresy of the inferiority of the sexual because they were afraid of women and marital duties. Heloise, the old reproaches you resort to when you resist the marriage with Abelard are really far fetched. For you the marriage was a bourgeois arrangement beneath the level of your spiritual, intellectual life. To be precise, far beneath Abelard's dignity. That was the actual reason for your refusal, Heloise: you feared the marriage would stand in the way of Abelard's career. It was and is customary that people expect a scholar to lead an exceptional life. But marriage means to lead a normal life, like everyone. And everyone knows the misery of married life. Heloise paints it in gray colors to her Abelard, who wants marriage: Marriage and academic work, she writes, are incompatible, because

no sooner are you deeply immersed in your theological and philosophical thoughts than the little children begin to bawl, their nurses try to put them to sleep with their monotonous singsong, the servants don't exactly work silently either, and you also don't want to turn up your nose when the children constantly need to be cleaned and have their diapers changed. . . . How can that go together: students and servants, your study and the nursery. . . . Rich people have spacious houses where someone can withdraw; their daily bread is not a problem for them, but a scholar . . .

A mere excuse: Abelard had enough money from his lecture fees to be able to afford a spacious home. Another excuse: His fame as a scholar would have been diminished by the marriage. When people found out about his secret marriage, was there a reduction in the number of his students? It increased. To be sure, as a married man he couldn't become a canon. By rights he couldn't become a priest either. But he did.

All of Heloise's objections were a house of cards. My suspicion is that she didn't want to get married. She didn't want a household. She wanted to lead the life of an intellectual. She didn't want a husband. She didn't want a crowd of children. She didn't even want me around her. But she wanted Abelard's love. She didn't want to be his wife, but rather, so she wrote, to be regarded as his whore. That probably means that everyone should recognize that she hadn't married Abelard in order to possess the famous man and build a nest with him, but that she loved him in all freedom, without any calculation and without wanting to disturb him in his work and require him to earn money. A love that was totally free is what she wanted.

Yes, but later, when he had sent her to the convent, she complained bitterly that he didn't visit her and didn't write to her. Admittedly, she says WE, she speaks of US, the nuns, but she means HERSELF.

Poor Mother, you weren't a genuine nun, you were and remain Abelard's beloved, you longed for his physical closeness, you dreamt of your past nights of love, you wanted to hear his vows of love, you were full of insatiable longing for the one you had lost. So did you want his pure friendship? What you wanted was to lie in his arms, to feel his hands (as in Fulbert's house in the past) on your bosom, his body on yours, that was it.

And how about Abelard? Why did he want the marriage? My suspicion is that he wanted to give full expression to his sensuality, legally, with his wedded wife, without committing the sin of fornication. Would the marriage really have disturbed him in his academic work? Heloise writes, quoting Seneca or some other of the ancients that they read together (his hand on her bosom – I can't get that image out of my mind! – his strong, slender hand grasping her bosom), that philosophy requires a whole person. Would Socrates have taught more and better things without his wife? Were all great teachers celibate, and did married people bring about nothing good? Did Paul owe his rhetorical genius to his celibacy? And didn't St. Jerome write his magnificent works although he moved around the country with a woman, Thekla (whom he called "his" and to whose presence "people simply had to resign themselves," in his own words)? And how was it with Aurelius Augustinus? Yes, how was that again. He was a professor of rhetoric in Carthage, then later of theology in Milan, and he had brought a girl along from his Africa with whom he lived for years in matrimonial companionship and with whom he had a child, Adeodatus, and in spite of all that he wrote magnificent books, and his beloved, child and all, didn't bother him; she stimulated him, and she protected him from indulging in excesses of a different kind. It was a great love. Whom did it bother? No one, except his mother, Monica, who had him since early childhood right under her thumb, followed him to Rome, lived with him, watched over him (she wasn't always successful in that), forced him to become a Christian, and thinking nothing of the loyal, monogamous love of the two lovers, chose a wife for him, whom he didn't love and with whom he had no intention of fathering a son. He didn't marry her, defying the will of his domineering mother, who without more ado sent his beloved back to Africa, but kept the grandson, who then died at seventeen. He was lucky. My brother in misfortune. Did you hate your parents? Why didn't you set off after your mother? Did your bigoted grandmother lock you up in Ostia? Wasn't your father man enough to free you, one way or another? Your father got his revenge in his own way: when his mother robbed him of his beloved, he no longer took care of his son; he began to go drinking and whoring. He writes that himself, he is very frank in his *Confessions*, not unlike my father, who took a certain delight in accusing himself of wicked things and secretly enjoyed them again while writing about them.

What happened to Augustine's repudiated companion? We don't know. But we know how he suffered. "My wound," so he wrote, "didn't heal; after the gnawing pain of the inflammation it began to rot, and its as it were now colder pain left all the less hope."

This mother, called a "saint," was a murderess. Her punishment was that her son did not marry the woman she ordered him to, he remained true to his African, from afar, founded a community of monks, and became a great teacher in the church.

Would he not have been one if he had been married or lived in cohabitation with his beloved? Perhaps he might not have written the *Confessions*. A great work of literature. But his main work about the Trinity would have been written in spite of everything. How strange that Augustine and Abelard describe the expression of their sexuality as a sin. Seven hundred years lie between the two! What pagan precepts: Gnostic and Manichaean have crept into a thoroughly misunderstood Christianity.

[70]

How did the abandoned women live? What did Augustine's beloved do? Did she commit suicide? Who knows.

What did Abelard's wife do? She is making a successful career for herself as prioress, she is capable, she looks after her "daughters" (instead of her son), she writes letters to her lover, the husband who now calls her the "bride of Christ," she reproaches him, she rails against God until Abelard, now the spiritual adviser of her convent, therefore also of her, forbids her this blasphemous complaining, and until she is quiet about it out of obedience and deep resignation, quiet forever. But what took place in her? She writes about it just as frankly as Abelard confesses his earlier sins. She writes (and calls on God as her witness, the God who was never fully real to her because her God is called Abelard): "Never have I sought anything else from you but you: *te pure, non tua concupiscens.*" I believe you, Mother Heloise. You have loved Abelard wholeheartedly, with body and soul, in complete devotion. I think only a woman loves like that. I don't wish to be loved like that or to love like that. Deprivation of personal liberty is what it is. Even years later in the convent you write to your lover that you dream of his embraces and feel impulses in your young body, impulses of a carnal nature. Well, now. That is natural. I doubt whether your prayers sufficed to satisfy you, although on the other hand I think I know your stubbornly ascetic severity and strength. I know, or at least people say so, that in women it isn't the physical gratification they actually long for, but the union with the loved person. Certainly it was the man, Abelard, who was keener on physical gratification. Men are like that. But he loved you nevertheless, Mother Heloise. He loved you as well as he could. He was and remains a man. He even describes how he, monk or not, in spite of mutilation and vow, his and hers, found the opportunity for secret embraces behind church pillars and in the dark shadow of the convent wall. There he could slip through a hole in the wall (I found it), when he preferred not to make a grand entrance legally through the gate, spiritual father of the nuns, adviser of the prioress, priest of the Church of the Paraclete. "Bride of Christ" he called his wife and thus committed the crime of adultery against the bridegroom Christ. He did it like everything else, without remorse, consistent with his teaching that the essence of sin is not the deed but the intention. Did he want to sin? No, he only wanted to love.

That doesn't appeal to me. I call it doing things by halves. One picks the apple, bites into it, and keeps the remains; one stays in the order, one renounces the marriage, one keeps one's good reputation in the world, one climbs up the career ladder – and robs for oneself secretly what was left to rob. So basically one hasn't lost much.

Heloise didn't have a guilty conscience. She didn't know what that was. She was radical. She stood by everything that she did. Not so with Abelard. His conscience tortured him fiendishly, and he finds sharp words when Heloise complains bitterly about what she lost and reproaches him, him and her (his) God. It didn't weigh heavily on either of them that it was a sin to abandon a child that they had brought into the world. "We left our child with my sister Denise," he writes. That's all. And much later she writes: "Dear friend Peter the Venerable, see that my son Astrolabe gets a position as canon." And a poem of Abelard's to me, in which he talks of "our" Heloise. What else? She pretended not to be in the Paraclete when I called. I went there several times, but when I was turned away the third time I contented myself with lying in the grass outside the wall, near the hole Abelard squeezed through. I never met him there. What would have happened if I had met him? I had the hunting knife in my pocket. One thrust, not from behind, but openly, from the front, well aimed, into his heart. Dying in my arms. His blood would come over me. Not out of hate did I kill you, but out of love; out of wild, jealous love for you and for my mother. Something like that. To cover your high forehead with kisses, and tears and blood on my face. And then? Kill myself with the same dagger? Or give myself up to a court of justice and tell the whole story? The guilt would fall on me alone. And Heloise's hatred too.

So not that.

I could have met him by chance, because he came to the Paraclete now and then. It was one of his duties to look after the convent. For Heloise's wishes he came all too seldom. She reproached him harshly. To be sure, she wrote of us, the nuns, but this us meant me. It wasn't the nuns who longed for him. It was Heloise who pined for him and wrote so very clearly. There is a letter that made me blush when I read it. She, the nun, still calls him her beloved, totally ignoring the fact that he is a monk and a priest and should therefore have finished with his past love. On the contrary: she reminds him of it again and again and demands his continued love, his exclusive love, which he is now allowed to have only for God. But that doesn't matter to her at all. This God is her enemy. He has robbed her of her beloved, of him and his love and her youth. Of what use to her are the pious letters that he occasionally writes to her and the nuns. She doesn't want pious speeches, she wants love, she wants to know that she is loved passionately, just as she loves passionately. What is her God and the whole world and even eternal bliss without him? You wrote such a letter, Mother Heloise:

If my self is not with you, then it is nowhere, and without you it has no meaning and essence. Let my heart be with you, please, please, and be protected by you. Oh, if only your love weren't able to rely so firmly on mine! If only you had to be more concerned! Now I have given you great assurance and have earned great disregard. Please don't forget what I have done for you, and also don't forget what you owe me. When I was allowed to enjoy the desires of the flesh while lying close to your heart, the world could doubt whether devoted love or selfish lust drove me into your arms. Now the end proves in which sense my love had its beginning: I have renounced all the pleasures of this world to be obedient to your will; I have given up everything and reserved only one thing for myself, to become entirely yours through this very sacrifice.

And you, you, take it to heart how unjust you are: My service is considerable, your service in return is not of the same magnitude, it is nothing. . . .

What does she actually demand of him? Nothing that he couldn't or wouldn't be allowed to give: letters. She reminds him how he wrote letter after letter at the time of the great passion of their love, and what letters, love songs to a name that all Paris knew, proud public professions of his love. And now this silence. Was his love dead?

Shouldn't you be reawakening God's love in me with a more perfect right than you previously awakened human desire in me? A last solemn request: think of your indebtedness and open your ears to my demand.

Those are hard words. She speaks of his guilt, she admits that he had seduced her, and now she derives her demand from that, a modest demand: to write to her. Really, that's the least he could do: write to her.

Finally he writes. His answer is a justification and is quite flimsy. He wants comfort from the one he should be comforting. He says she doesn't need his advice and encouragement, because she herself is intelligent and strong, she sustains the weak, teaches the wayward, comforts the faint of heart.

He himself is the person who needs advice and help. He speaks of his enemies, who are trying to kill him. The letter reads like a last will and testament.

If the Lord lets me fall into the hands of my enemies, so that they kill me, then I ask and implore of you: Wherever my body lies below or above the earth, have it brought back to your graveyard.

Who is after his life? Who wants to kill him? He doesn't mention names, but speaks of "grave danger, which worries him." He always feels that he is being followed, sometimes rightly so by actual enemies, but often, I think, it was his own daemon that drove him and sensed persecutors where there were none, and where there were none, he created them for himself, as in Saint-Denis.

But then he really did seem to have been in danger; if not in mortal danger, then in a situation that for him was worse than loss of life: the loss of his honor and his reputation as a great orthodox teacher of theology. It concerned his work "On the Divine Unity and Trinity." He had written it for his students who, spurred on by his influence, were tired of just parroting incomprehensible words to pass the exams and wanted really to understand what they heard. That is to say, they wanted philosophical proofs for their belief. They said their teachers were the blind leading the blind. Abelard wasn't primarily a theologian, but a philosopher, and so he was used to working with logic and dialectics. That was something new and filled the students with enthusiasm, but not his colleagues, naturally not. Something new of that sort is suspicious just because it's new. It shakes traditions, it forces debates. That's uncomfortable. This Abelard was dangerous. Was he even a theologian? He was a philosopher and had no permission to teach theology. What did he understand of it? His permission to teach would have to be taken away. The permission to teach anything, not just theology, because this eloquent, cunning teacher with countless tricks up his sleeve was capable of smuggling in his heresies unnoticed under the cloak of orthodox phrases. Action would have to be taken against him, publicly. The man would have to be destroyed, once and for all, before he infected an entire generation of young people with his heresies.

They asked Abelard to come before the synod in Soissons. His enemies had been so good at their subversive activities that even the common people, who didn't have a clue what it was about, were set against this Abelard. He and some of his loyal students actually had stones thrown at them on the way to Soissons. Did the stupid people know what a great mind they were aiming at?

I ask myself whether I, had I already been one of his students then, would have had the courage to go with him. I would do it today. But that is easily said. At the time I was a child, three years old, I played under the Breton apple trees with kittens and lambs and blocks of wood, called Denise *Maman*, was happy, and had no idea that I had a father who was summoned before an ecclesiastical court because he had written a book that contained things all too new and sublime for his callous colleagues to be able to understand. They (if I can believe your account of your life, Father – you exaggerate sometimes, as I now know) actually wanted to have him burned at the stake, him or his books, which would have meant the same to him, namely, the end of his career. It turned out differently. It always turned out differently in his life.

In any case, I read in your account of your life, Abelard, that you obeyed the summons to Soissons and brought along the offensive work on the Trinity, quite prepared to correct any heresies and even to do penance. Did you mean that seriously, Father? Were you sure that you hadn't written a single heresy? Or rather were you sure that with your brilliant talent for thinking and speaking you could refute every objection to your teaching, regardless of how close it might be to heresy? Did you know not only the hostile malice of your adversaries, Alberich and Ludolf, but also their intellectual inferiority?

[75]

Did you know that in a duel of words you could beat them flat with your polished arguments? And yet you felt miserable. Things could also end badly, because when had reason ever triumphed over blind malice? You begged your wife, your sister bride (as you called her), for help through her prayers and those of her convent. You thought highly of her prayer or, shall we say, of the great power of her love. I'm convinced that she – who otherwise didn't think much of God, since he had robbed her of her Abelard, youth, sensuality, and freedom – was on her knees day and night sending strength to her beloved.

The Synod of Soissons took a strange course. Quite against every rule, Abelard's prosecutors were also his judges, and they were his deadly enemies. The papal legates, though, had already read the book, as had the archbishop, and then it went like the court proceedings of Jesus before Pilate: no one found him guilty. At first. The synod dragged on, and Abelard used the time to hold public lectures on the contentious topic. Naturally he had many listeners, and they asked themselves what he was saying that was heretical. Everything was orthodox and well said. It had to end in an acquittal.

But Abelard's enemies couldn't accept that. What a disgrace. The devil had to be found at any cost in all that Abelardian orthodoxy. Alberich found him. Abelard's archenemy suddenly turned up among those present in the company of several students. Then the cloven hoof came out: Abelard had written that God had begotten God; but that wasn't possible, since there is only One God. Abelard writes in his *Life Confession* that he was prepared to interpret the sentence rationally. Alberich said that reason had nothing to say in such questions; what mattered was only the stated views of the church fathers. He hadn't counted on Abelard being so very well read. Abelard opened Augustine's chapter on the Trinity and immediately found the right place, which reads: "Whoever believes that God has the power to beget himself is very much mistaken; this capability does not befit God; it does not befit any spiritual or bodily creature at all."

When I later once read this passage aloud to my father professor, I said, There is a linguistic mistake here. The word creature is quite unsuitable and not applicable to God; whoever does so slips into heresy without knowing it; the category creature can't be used to define God. Whoever does so is maintaining that God is one of his own creatures.

But when Abelard had his argument with Alberich, I was a child who only fought with wooden sabres and a few coarse swearwords I had picked up.

At that time in Soissons, Abelard won a victory over Alberich. The synod members found no heresy in Abelard's writings, but didn't want to admit defeat. However, there was one sensible man there, Bishop Godfrey of Chartres, whose words carried weight. Whether or not he was really convinced of Abelard's immaculate orthodoxy, he was in any case clever enough to avoid a scandal. Abelard was famous and had too many followers for anyone to invite the hatred of so many and risk being regarded as envious of him. Besides, a condemnation of his writings would only increase Abelard's fame and bring a large number of defenders onto the scene. Godfrey's advice was to bring Abelard before a public council and put questions to him that he was to answer in such a way that it would be clearly recognizable whether or not he was a heretic. But then his enemies wrote (Abelard recorded it as follows): "We are supposed to fight with this hero of words who makes the whole world succumb to him with his sophistic proofs?" The bishop was not so much trying to stand by Abelard as to save his honor and that of the synod members. He wanted to convene a council, one with "real" experts, as he said. That was a slap in the face of Abelard's enemies, whom he accused of incompetence. In addition, he wanted to move the location of the council out of the Diocese of Reims. But he was shouted down.

It is moving to read in Abelard's *Story of My Misfortunes* that he unexpectedly found a friend in the Bishop of Chartres, who advised him to undergo the test with humility; it would only last a few days, he would finally have to be acquitted because the machinations of his enemies were all too clearly transparent. But those enemies were strong. They pushed through a decree that he personally had to throw his book into the fire. He did it. One of his pupils, who had been there, later told me that the fire burned up straight as a candle, that there was no wind at all, that the charred pages fell very gently back to earth, and that Abelard held his hand out flat to catch a still burning

[77]

page and let it burn completely in his hand without showing any sign of pain. Indeed, he had a reddish spot in the palm of his right hand that I later saw myself, it never disappeared.

The scene took place in deep silence until a voice said quietly, Fair punishment for a heresy; in Abelard's book it says that only God the Father is omnipotent.

The papal legate heard that and said in all innocence, But we know that there are three omnipotent beings.

Then a courageous student called Terricus called out, Does it not say in the Athanasian Creed that there is only one omnipotent being?

People rebuked him, but he called out: You have damned a person before you found out the facts of the matter! You appointed someone who was mistaken himself to fight against a mistake. Abelard is innocent!

That made an impression on some, and the archbishop decided that they should have Abelard recite the Athanasian Creed, then they would see whether he rightfully believed.

How humiliating for Abelard, the great theologian, to be expected to do exactly what he fought against in his students: to repeat words like a parrot. He wanted, as was his way, to interpret the text. They cut him short. They tested him orally on the creed like a schoolboy. Not enough: they feared that he could cunningly leave out or add this word or that unnoticed. They pressed a piece of paper into his hand from which he had to read the creed. He did so in tears with a choking voice.

I am ashamed of this scene even today. Why didn't he keep silent? Why did he accept the humiliation? Why did he let them see him cry? Mustn't his enemies have taken these tears as tears of remorse? In your place, Father, I would have shown the pack my contempt right to their faces, and my superiority. If they had let you talk, how brilliantly you could have proven to them that you have penetrated more deeply into the secret of the Trinity than any of these timid, stupid, narrow-minded traditionalists ever could. I wouldn't have put up with this injustice. I would have mobilized all my friends and students. I would have appealed to the pope. I would have demanded proper legal proceedings, a council with experts, as the bishop of Chartres wanted. What happened to you, Abelard? Why this weakness? Was it tiredness, was it humility, or what was it?

You left Soissons like one defeated and went to Saint-Médard as if to jail, like a heretic being transferred there.

When I was your student, Father, you once asked me what I thought about that disputed issue. I said, Although God is triune, he is nevertheless One, and in this One each of the Three has his special characteristics. Naturally all Three are omnipotent, but we, who know only ancillary words, attribute the omnipotence to him we call the Father. But this omnipotence is also active in the other two persons. If we don't attribute the omnipotence also to the Son and to the Holy Ghost, we rob them of their divinity, because omnipotence is part of divinity.

Abelard listened silently, as was his way, then he slapped me on the shoulder, You don't know how carefully one has to handle such statements.

This fleeting touch: was it a sign of caring? It almost seemed so. My heart was pounding. It was during the time that we had not yet revealed ourselves to each other as father and son.

But I have gotten far ahead of myself. What happened to Abelard after the sentencing in Soissons?

As always in his life it turned out differently than expected. The Saint-Médard monastery was supposed to be a prison for heretics. But the abbot was proud to have the great Abelard within his walls. He treated him honorably, and he and all the monks tried to console him. In vain. He was all too deeply hurt. It was the second great humiliation that the proud, haughty man had suffered. He considered the first, the castration, a just punishment, but the second an injustice that cried out to heaven. He knew that he was in the right before his highest authority, his logically thinking mind, which he knew to be in complete agreement with real faith, that is, with what man is able to know of the divine. He suffered inordinately. The abbot saw him suffer and suffered with him. He secretly admired Abelard and found it outrageous to detain the great mind in a penal monastery. He was ashamed to be considered one of those people like Ludolf and Alberich, Abelard's wily enemies. He persuaded the abbot of Saint-Denis to admit Abelard again into his parent monastery; with good reason, since in the meantime the papal legate declared that Abelard had been rashly and unjustly condemned at the instigation of Ludolf and Alberich. They, of course, beat their breasts and swore they had nothing to do with the matter. Miserable, cowardly fellows.

It soon became apparent that Abelard's return to Saint-Denis wreaked new havoc. Abelard could well believe it: ever since he first entered the order, the monks hadn't been able to stand him. He was a provocation: a famous scholar among barely mediocre minds, a great character among average folk, someone who had become a strict ascetic and had taken it upon himself to bring the demoralized monastery back to its former height. He! He of all people, the newcomer, the eunuch, he with his notorious love story.

They had been very glad when he had been transferred. And now he was back again, in fact rehabilitated, although forbidden to teach. But that wouldn't last long, one could already foresee that. Students were already applying. They had to be turned away. They rebelled. They held a sit-in in front of the monastery gate. They called for Abelard until they were driven away by the threat that they would be reported to the king. Nevertheless, some of them came again and again. There was no teacher in all of Paris who could have replaced Abelard.

And at the same time the rumor persisted that Abelard was having secret talks with the abbot about radically reforming the monastery.

If people had thought that Abelard had returned home as a seriously wounded lion, they found that he wasn't so easily destroyed. They feared him, they would have feared even the paws of the dead lion. They had no idea how much he suffered. He kept everything to himself. He led an exemplary life. That was a provocation. With his silent, pious austerity, without saying or doing anything, this man brought the monastery into an uproar.

They had to get rid of him. But how?

Poor Father, again you played right into your enemies' hands.

At first, this stern monk gave not the slightest cause for hostilities. He worked from early to late in the large library. He had been forbidden to teach, but not forbidden to research and to write. The only requirement was that none of his writings be allowed to enter the public domain; there were already far too many of his writings in circulation. It hadn't helped a bit that his work on the Trinity had been burned in Soissons. Several of his students had copied it out beforehand. The copies circulated and were copied again, and no ban could hinder it. Even if no written page had remained: Abelard's words, once spoken, would have remained as if carved in stone. Books can be burned, but not the spirit. It lives, loved or feared, denounced or canonized by the church.

But what happened that made Abelard fear for his life, as he wrote to Heloise? I heard the story from several sides and at different times, and it seemed more and more absurd to me. If I wrote comedies, I'd write a play about it that would make the audience pee in their pants for laughter. For only with laughter could one have answered this foolish historical argument.

And that is how Abelard understood it: he laughed. He laughed seldom, but then he laughed loudly. This merry, mocking laughter brought him embittered enemies, who wanted to bring the matter before the king. A lèse-majesté, a disparagement of the dignity of the Kingdom of France. How, in what way? Several dozen old bones were to blame, bones that had been found when the crypt of the church was under reconstruction and that people thought were the mortal remains of the great Dionysius the Areopagite. Even this expression was an insult to the monastery. What does that mean: people thought they were? They were. What did opinion have to do with it? It was, after all, a historically proven fact. People knew that the great Greek theologian and mystic was the patron saint or even the founder of the monastery. He had lived in the first or second century, had been a disciple of the apostle Paul and had become bishop of Athens. People believed. And people believed that he personally had written the famous works that were, without checking, attributed to the "Areopagite." No one asked how this Greek had come in the flesh or even as a skeleton to Paris, and people took care not to ask that. Until Abelard came, the accursed, stubborn questioner, the rationalist, the honest academic. He hadn't even asked, but rather the question and answer fell into his hands in the library when he was leafing through a work by the Venerable Bede, the English historian. It said there that Dionysius the Areopagite was a pseudonym, perhaps for an entire team of authors or, if only for one, for the bishop of Corinth, not of Athens.

Now what difference did that make? To Abelard actually no difference, but what irritated him was the historical inexactness and the obstinate adherence to a tradition. Even worse, the shameless financial exploitation of a tradition proven to be wrong – the bones found in the crypt were shown to the pious people as those of the great monastery founder Dionysius the Areopagite. The people believed it and held the bones in great honor as relics. In practice it meant that many people came flocking to the monastery, expecting the saint to perform miracles, and supporting their prayers with donations that benefited the monastery; the entire monastery lived from these contributions and from the fame of having the great Dionysius the Areopagite as its founder or patron saint. A legend had long since become history. Abelard found out what it meant to shake it. Of course it had to be Abelard. Couldn't he leave the matter alone? Whom did it harm? No one. But it did harm the truth and the dependable honor of academic work.

For once, Abelard had not sought out this scandal for himself; no one had set the fox trap for him, he had gotten into it unawares. Who guided his hand when he pulled a book by the Venerable Bede from the shelf? Who had him open the page on which Bede, the great, exact historian, maintained that the Areopagite was not the bishop of Athens but the bishop of Corinth? How could Abelard know that Bede was right? How did he know so much about the Areopagite? And why at this moment did he have an uncontrollable desire to laugh? And why did a clever young student who was interested in Abelard's laughter just happen to be in the library? And why did Abelard talk with him about a matter of complete indifference that nevertheless contained the material for a comedy?

Yes, why? That's just the way it was. Abelard's daemon wanted it.

The monk didn't know there had been an argument about this Areopagite. Abbot Hilduin, perhaps knowing Bede, had travelled to Greece to find the traces of the Areopagite, and he found them; naturally he found them where he wanted to find them. He returned with the firm belief that the Areopagite was the bishop of Athens. That very Dionysius the Areopagite probably didn't exist at all as a person, but rather was named as the author of a series of mystical writings. Everything seemed clear: the monastery had as its founder a great theologian and saint.

The monk who had heard Abelard's laughter told me that Abelard said, Look here, you can read something here that would taste rough to the abbot, and not only to him. We'll probably have to be satisfied with less great a founder. As it turns out, we can't get away with saying a disciple of the apostle Paul is the founder.

But if Bede is wrong?

Read this page, it's a quotation attributed to the Areopagite; read it word for word. I'll give you an hour's time to make a great discovery.

The monk told me, I didn't need an hour to find out that words, concepts, ideas were used there that turned up for the first time in the fifth and sixth centuries. The language is Neoplatonic. A disciple of the apostle Paul could never have written like that. Moreover there are turns of speech that make the text seem old and artificially antiquated words; an educated person can't help noticing that. Abelard was delighted. Good thinking, he said, but where do you see the proof that the bones in the crypt are not those of the Areopagite and therefore rightly honored as relics?

Doesn't the proof lie in the fact that he did not even exist?

Can you prove that he didn't exist? You see, you can't do that. You can prove that the writings that are considered here in the monastery to be authentic works by the Greek called Dionysius the Areopagite can't come from this man. Of course only scholars who have made an exact study of the works of the Areopagite and who accept comparative philology as a philosophical method will accept this proof. I'd really like to write an article about it. I could probably also prove that as far as the founder of our monastery is concerned, it's simply a case of mistaken identity. The founder was certainly called Dionysius. There are a number of theologians with that name, but I suspect that our man is the Dionysius who was a bishop in Paris and who was killed as a martyr in the sixth century. It's plausible that his bones were brought here.

[83]

But why do people here insist that not this Dionysius is the founder, but rather that one who can't possibly be?

Why? Because the other one, if he existed as a person, is much more famous, and only the most famous of all is good enough for us. The king above all insists that only he has the Areopagite as a patron saint and that these are the very bones of the Areopagite.

Yes, but if these bones do work miracles, then one could say openly whose they are.

So you think. But it would be a shame to admit that one had made a mistake. A king and a bishop never make mistakes, don't forget that.

I understand. If one said the simple truth, the pious people would feel betrayed and wouldn't come anymore. What would be the monastery's source of income then?

We laughed uncontrollably, the monk told me. Although he belonged to the monastery, he was still young enough to have retained a trace of secular rebelliousness. And he had a sense of humor. He said he found the story funny and acted it out in front of Abelard. He played the Venerable Bede reading a text aloud from a book, some highly learned text that he, the student, made up as he read aloud. Then he, as Bede, had to defend himself against a mob of angry people who called him a liar, a swindler, an enemy of the church, an enemy of the monastery. Screaming and stamping, the student enacted the part of the monks gone wild. Sudden quiet. He stares at the floor; all seem horrified. The student acted out the scene in front of me as he had acted it out in front of Abelard. God help us! he called as the cover of the grave rises and a skeleton climbs out and asks in an archaic language what is going on, why people are bothering him; he wants his rest, he is the brother cook, who came here with Bishop Dionysius from Paris in the year 580.

He took me with him because he was afraid of being poisoned by the monks here. I was supposed to cook and sample the food in advance for him, my bishop. I did that well. But one morning when I came into the kitchen there was a pitcher of wine there, the pitcher that was reserved for the abbot of the monastery; it had come fresh from the cellar and smelled so irresistible that I drank some. Yes, and then I fell down and have been dead ever since. Who had put the poison in the pitcher? Who was really supposed to be poisoned there? The abbot of the monastery? Certainly not I, the poor brother cook. God could not punish me so cruelly for the desires of my taste buds and the trivial theft. Oh, if only I hadn't drunk, oh, if only I had restrained my desire, I would have returned unharmed with my bishop to Paris. To be sure, they soon killed him there. Now they worship him as a martyr. And me too.

Abelard laughed until he cried. That laughter almost cost him his life. For he and the young monk had listeners. There were always a few spies lurking around Abelard. One day one of them asked him if he knew what Abbot Hilduin said about Dionysius the Areopagite and whether he agreed with him or with the impertinent Englishman Bede. Abelard smelled a rat but thought he could adroitly sidestep the issue by saying that Bede was a great authority for the entire Church, so one would have to trust him. Already too much said, already too clear. They informed Abbot Hilduin of Abelard's words. I'm certain today that by doing so they put Hilduin in a tricky situation.

What should he do? The abbot valued Abelard, who was actually the showpiece of his monastery, even if a dubious, disreputable one. But for all that, it was bad to abandon him. Bad for the reputation of the monastery too. On the other hand, to assert that the great Dionysius the Areopagite was not the patron saint of the Kingdom of France was an attack on the honor and credibility of the royal tradition, indeed, on the person of the king. Wasn't that lèse-majesté? Didn't that come close to high treason? If Hilduin let the matter rest, he made himself Abelard's tacit accomplice and risked being punished himself. If he conceded that Abelard was right and cited the Venerable Bede, then that meant that he put Bede in an unfavorable light, indeed, declared him a falsifier of history. By doing so, though, he would have made a fool of himself to the historians, for whom Bede was the indisputable academic authority. In addition, he would have made enemies of the English, since Bede was an Englishman.

Hilduin wanted to help Abelard and keep him, but how? He hoped for something from a conversation with the great dialectician. He would get himself out of the trap. He could shoot every one of their arguments to pieces. Admittedly, though, the king was no academic open to sensible arguments, but rather an obstinate ruler who wasn't concerned with historical argumentation but with sacred tradition, even if it was based on obvious fallacies. In that case one simply says: I, the king, or I, the bishop, or I, the pope want it that way, and therefore that's the way it is. Might is always right.

Hadn't Abelard spoken at the Synod of Soissons "in diverse tongues," as it says in the Bible, and didn't everyone believe him, and wasn't he still condemned? And among those who sat in judgment on him there were at least some scholars. But before the king Abelard would always be the loser, because nobody would dare to concede that he was right instead of the king.

Abelard was trapped. Literally. Before he was officially tried in the royal court, he was locked up in a cell. The fate of many great people, to land in jail. The proven means of silencing unpleasant troublemakers.

Poor Abelard. Your fate, your character: wherever you went, you quickly realized what was going on and created a disturbance and put yourself in danger.

At that time you were aware of your situation, you exaggerated it perhaps in that you feared even for your life. You wrote a prayer then that Heloise and her nuns were asked to say for you:

Do not forsake me, God, Father and Lord of our life, that I may not break down before the eyes of my adversaries and that my enemy may not triumph over me.

Did Abelard really fear he would be condemned to death or maliciously murdered? Neither of the two was out of the question. Hilduin was cowardly, a servant of the king, and even if he didn't clearly admit it to himself: Abelard was a thorn in his flesh, a constant nuisance, a living reproach for the bad management of the monastery.

The simplest thing would have been to lure Abelard into the woods and have him abducted, killed, and buried somewhere by hired thugs. Under no circumstances must this Abelard be made into a martyr. Because he would be that. His students and several powerful friends would see to it. So not that. If only this blasted Abelard would just disappear of his own accord!

And he did disappear, some of his former students helped him flee under cover of darkness and also rescued Abelard's important works.

But where to go now? How far did Abbot Hilduin's power reach, how far did the king's?

At first Abelard was sheltered. Nearby was the territory belonging to Count Theobald, who owned Provins Castle. The count admired Abelard. He took him in with pleasure and gave him a place where he could live in seclusion. But he didn't have peace and quiet. Abelard still felt unsafe. He always reckoned with enemies and with death. He wrote to Heloise at that time that she should bury his body in the graveyard of her convent. I am moved by this request. Actually, for a devout Christian (and my father was that: deeply religious, and for that very reason the "believers" considered him a heretic) it doesn't matter where his bodily remains are laid to rest. But Abelard wanted to go to Heloise. He wanted to sleep beside her. He needed her company even in death. In all eternity

For myself, I wish to return home at last to my mother. To lie as a dead child in her lap. To lie with my father and mother in eternal peace, accepted and loved by both of them forever.

I've never dared to express this wish, not even to our best friend, Peter the Venerable. I'm certain he would have respected my wish. But my parents? Would they want me? Have they ever wanted me? Wasn't I always an unnecessary person? Nothing but the fruit of a wild passion. They were sufficient unto themselves. Why force myself between them in death or even seek their company? Well, it's all the same to me where I am buried. I would like best to have a grave in Pallet. If ever I had a home, then it was there, in my childhood, when I knew nothing of my ill-fated origins.

But back to that interval in which Abelard could rest a little. Outwardly. Inwardly he was tormented by his treatment in Saint-Denis. He felt that he belonged there. In spite of everything.

One day his abbot, Hilduin, came to see Count Theobald. And now Abelard did something that I, who am so much more insignificant in comparison, would never have done: he asked the abbot for forgiveness.

Yes, damn it, why? Because he, as a scholar, loved the truth above all else?

This request for forgiveness is beneath Abelard. What was his offense? People say he offended against monastic rule. How so? Because he had dared to think for himself and to say what he thought. Because he encroached on the abbot's authority. Because he laughed at the absurdity of the dispute about the old bones. Because he was himself, completely himself.

But now to eat humble pie. Is that Abelard? That is a clerically broken man. Someone who is afraid of people who can't hold a candle to him as far as intellect and innate dignity are concerned. People who for their part are afraid of his sharp intellect.

How often he has already been wounded, and how deeply, and now suddenly he sinks to his knees. I'm ashamed for my father. I'm ashamed that he did not leave that monastery, that order. I'm also ashamed for Abbot Hilduin, who asked for time for reflection before he granted Abelard "forgiveness."

Abelard no longer wanted to go back to Saint-Denis. Wasn't that what they also wanted in Saint-Denis: to be rid of the aggravating monk?

But if Abelard wanted to leave Saint-Denis in order to enter another monastery? That would be an insult to Saint-Denis, a public criticism. That couldn't be allowed. Therefore the absurd thing happened: they refused Abelard what they themselves wanted. They threatened him with excommunication if he didn't return. Abelard's fate: the sudden turn of events. Hardly had the abbot returned to Saint-Denis, when he died. How would his successor behave? Again the twist of Abelard's fate: He who was threatened with the king's verdict found friends just there, at the king's court. Calculating friends, of course. They told the king that Abelard didn't fit in at Saint-Denis. Why not? That they didn't say. In Saint-Denis they led a lax life but were loyal to the king, and presumably they delivered considerable riches from the monastery to the court.

So Abelard was no longer to go to Saint-Denis, but neither to any other monastery. Where to go?

Where he wanted and how he wanted to live. They had gotten generous. Perhaps they had a bad conscience. Friends gave him a piece of land, and on it he built that chapel he first dedicated to the Trinity, but then called

"Paraclete." Paraclete: the Comforter, the Holy Ghost. Here he resolved to live as a hermit and to study, free of worldly cares and compulsions. He lived in great poverty. Word got around. Students tracked him down and cared for him. All of them lived in poverty, even the sons of rich people. They fled from the temptations of the big city and its diversions. They wanted nothing but to study, and that with the best teacher there was. More and more students, more and more suspicions among his colleagues. What's going on there in the woods? They infiltrated the group with spies. Their reports brought nothing bad to light. Some of the spies even stayed, attracted by the new way of living and working.

But wasn't something highly dangerous in progress there? Didn't it have something to do with the plans that were secretly going around about church reform? There were these new ideas about living in voluntary poverty, about the radical imitation of Christ, about renouncing every kind of privilege. That was open criticism of the Church and its wealth and its abuse of power. That was, clearly, the beginning of a revolution. What does the imitation of Christ mean here? We live in different times. We are not poor, uneducated Hebrews. We are gentlemen. And we have a right to property, to gifts, to a life of luxury. Whoever touches that is an enemy of the church. An enemy of the faith. It amounts to the same thing. Whoever criticizes the Church is criticizing Christianity, undermining the authority appointed by Christ. This Abelard is capable of anything. His influence on the young people is very strong. They run after him like sheep, but he turns them into rams.

And isn't there that Italian, Arnold of Brescia? Hadn't the Second Lateran Council of 1139 banished him from his Italian homeland because of heretical ideas? Abelard got his ideal of poverty from him. Or vice versa. In any case, these two are in league. Hadn't this Italian accused the Church of selling the freedom of God's children for money, benefices, lavish gifts, privileges? What did all this criticism by the young hotheads lead to? To stirring up the people. To inciting the common people against the clergy and therefore against any authority. That meant that they would want to take away from the clergy some of its property made sacrosanct by tradition. Wasn't this Italian openly denouncing the wealth of the Church? Wasn't he saying loudly enough that the clergy spoke the words of the imitation of Christ, but their lifestyle was utterly unchristian? A dangerous rebellion was brewing in the woods. At any rate, a generation of theologians was being bred there that was to be feared. Weren't the foundations of the church shaking already?

The moderate among the clergy only found it highly offensive that a single man was taking hundreds of students away from regular, controlled, censored university training and was emptying the Paris lecture halls. Shouldn't this whole suspicious business be stopped before it was too late? After all, the young people were already infected with the sickness of thinking and were grumbling about the dictate of blind faith. This Abelard was the igniting spark. There was enough flammable material available. Finally one of Abelard's enemies found the welcome occasion to denounce him. What had Abelard called the church of his school in the woods? The Paraclete. Not the Holy Trinity? Only one of the three persons, the Holy Ghost. There was an old heresy hidden in that, an attack on the unity of the Trinity. To consecrate a church to the Holy Ghost alone was to deny this unity by singling out one person.

Poor Abelard, how they maliciously misunderstood you. Of course you meant the entirety of the Trinity but addressed that side of this triunity that was most important to you at the moment, the Holy Ghost, the Comforter. He was in dire need of the Paraclete.

Naturally Abelard could have defended himself: It is no heresy to dedicate a festival to one of the three divine persons. Why shouldn't one also dedicate a chapel to one of them? The whole Trinity was always what was meant. In his *Story of My Misfortunes* he emphasizes that with "Paraclete" he had meant the whole Trinity. But I suspect that the Holy Ghost was something very special for him. I remember Jesus' sentence from the Gospel: "I will send you another Comforter who will teach you everything." That meant that Jesus had not yet revealed everything and that someone who was yet to come would do so, albeit he had always been there, since he lived within the Trinity. Abelard dared to break new ground: He believed in a continuation of the revelation. He believed in a development. He believed that thought would always provide new openings. But for him thought meant not only rational argumentation, it meant awakening greater and greater human potential for interpreting the revelation in its various phases. Something spreading out like a fan, so to speak. It took me a long time to understand that for him thought meant listening more and more attentively to the *one* unfolding revelation. So he could probably believe in the Paraclete as one of the persons of the Trinity, but also regard it as the principle of the evolution of the whole.

When I once spoke about it later with Abelard, my father, he said, It's better that you keep this opinion of yours to yourself; the time isn't ripe yet for this thought. And bear in mind that to fight for a new interpretation is to draw up and sign your own death warrant!

Do you think I'm a coward, father?

No. But look at me: I'm strong, you aren't as strong, and if the might of the church has already broken me, how would you fare? We were born too early. Or else several centuries too late. Dionysius the Areopagite would have understood us.

There was that name again, that man or rather the works attributed to him that meant so much to Abelard. I only understood that when the young monk who had helped Abelard during his flight by night from Saint-Denis slipped me those pages that were covered with notes in Abelard's handwriting.

I later handed them over to Peter the Venerable; I had made copies for myself. They are sacred to me. In them I find him whom I call Father, albeit with the old bitter taste in my mouth.

I'm enclosing some of these pages for you, Mother Heloise. Others were too important to me to let them out of my hands. There are some that refer to Abelard's work on the Trinity. One can see how many years he occupied himself with this topic. It seems as if the dispute about Dionysius the Areopagite was the stimulus for special studies.

I'm sending you excerpts of several notes about that, only such as undoubtedly stem from Abelard's hand, but were copied by me.

Dionysius, bishop of Corinth, second century. Dionysius, patriarch of Syria, ninth century, wrote a great historical work and came to an agreement with the Muslims so that they stopped their attacks on the Christians. Dionysius of Alexandria, who was accused by a pope of the same name of preaching a heretical doctrine of the Trinity. (Abelard: was persecuted, had to flee, was banned, late comeback. The same old song.) Dionysius of Milan: stood up bravely at the Council of Milan against Emperor Constantine II, who encouraged the heresy of the Arians; Arius's doctrine of the Trinity: God is not created and not begotten. The Son, the Logos, is not identical in nature to the Father and is by no means the true God. He is not identical to the Logos of the Father. He is God only through communion with God, exactly as we are. The Son is not identical to the Father, only similar to him.

Further back in time: in the third century a Dionysius, pupil of Origen. Abelard notes in the margin of the page:

Idea of spiritual struggle. Mysticism and ascent of the mountain: ascent of the soul to virtue and mystical insight. Sees the bride in the Song of Solomon as the soul that glows with longing to see God. Ideal of virginity. Asceticism.

A separate page about Origen:

Asceticism. Literal interpretation of Matthew 19.12. Is a man allowed to send away his wife for any reason? The Pharisees' question to Jesus. His answer: What God has brought together, let no man rend asunder. The disciples: If that's how the matter stands, it's not good to marry. Jesus' answer: There are celibates who were made incapable of marriage by other people, and there are celibates who remain celibate for the sake of the kingdom of heaven.

Abelard's marginal note about that: "Origen's self-castration; conclusive deadening of carnal desire." A number of similar observations on the topic of celibacy and asceticism.

My question to you, Father Abelard: When the organ of temptation is no longer there, then asceticism can surely no longer be a virtue; it's simply a natural consequence of a deficiency. My further question: Was Origen after his castration (his voluntary self-mutilation) still a man? Of what does his masculinity consist? It seems to me that Origen remained a man inasmuch as he fought his enemies like a man.

Abelard mentions yet another Dionysius who, he notes, "was an important conveyor of Oriental, Greek, and Latin intellectual culture." Here in Abelard's hand: "*Sic.* Hel." What does that mean? Hel? Heloise. Presumably she, who was familiar with Greek and Latin literature, had read the writings of this Dionysius. Presumably, together with Abelard, no, certainly. Between the theological pages another page, written with different ink and in less careful handwriting; only the year is written carefully: 1118. It was during that time that Heloise was Abelard's student in Fulbert's house. And it says now quite honestly in his *Story of My Misfortunes*:

During the lessons we had plenty of time for our love; unlike lovers longing to find a quiet place, we needed only to retire to immerse ourselves in our studies. The books lay there open, question and answer came urgently when love was the preferred topic, and there were more kisses than words. My hand had more to seek on her bosom than in the book. . . . .

Abelard was a match for the great Augustine in confessing his sins with relish. But I am suffocating in my jealousy. I am nothing but jealous. I understand every murderer who acts out of jealousy. Just get rid of the rival . . .

But what the hell am I writing here? When Abelard was grasping Heloise's bosom with his long, strong, beautiful hands, where was I then? How could I be a rival, being yet unborn? And yet, I was. From time immemorial I was, I am, I remain one. The image of Abelard's hands on my mother's bosom — that is a hellish picture. This bosom is that of my mother, it belongs to me, not to him. It served him for his desire, but it served me for nourishment. To me it was nest and refuge. I couldn't live without it. But he could. He only used it for his desire. And she, she nestled her firm, young bosom in his hands.

I have to murder Abelard or myself. One of us must die.

There are said to be fathers who are jealous of their own sons. If Abelard had known how often I wanted to sleep with his wife in incest, in a dream, in my imagination. . . . But even there there was a barrier, even there this Abelard lay there before me. Wherever I went, he had already been there. Whatever I wanted he had already taken for himself. Whatever I wanted to do, he had already done. Whatever I wanted to be, he had long since been. All the places in my life were occupied by Abelard.

[93]

Back to the pages that the young monk had rescued from Saint-Denis. There was a page there with notes that, in connection with the Areopagite, dealt with Montanus. I read: "Once a priest of Apollo or Cybele. Participation of women in the church. Rejection of the *jus docendi* of women in the church."

In the margin in Abelard's hand again: "*Sic.* Hel." Did the young Heloise have the right to teach? Were those words of rejection, written hundreds of years ago, still in force? Perhaps Heloise could only teach privately? The right to lecture at the university was probably denied her, even though she was, not only in Abelard's opinion, more qualified for it than most of the teachers.

Then a note against miracles and magical cures as proof of the divinity of Jesus Christ: To beg for magical help for oneself from God is crude magic. Quotation from Dionysius the Areopagite, who himself was a great mystic, but rejected mystical-magical practices. Nevertheless, the meaning of the Paraclete: loss of consciousness of the self as the condition for the streaming in of the Holy Ghost.

For me it is very difficult to reconcile Abelard's appreciation of mysticism with his rationality. Can a true scholar actually deal with something that can't be grasped by ratiocination? The same problem: How can one believe what cannot be proven, that is: How can one occupy oneself with God, who is fully unrecognizable? How can one study theology as one studies medicine? The bridge must be philosophy. But does it hold? It bears its own weight, but can one get to the other shore on it? I had the feeling that one could either not recognize God at all, not even through a hundred years of studies, or else he reveals himself in a single moment. Except that what one then knows of him cannot be communicated.

But these questions were quite unimportant to me for a while. Something had changed again in Abelard's life: they had given him back the permission to teach; he was now a teacher at the university on the Sainte-Geneviève Mountain in Paris and naturally had a full lecture hall again. Our relationship was still unclear. The semester began, and this Abelard, marked by the tribulations he had suffered, stood again behind the lectern, and it was clear that he was deliberately overlooking me. At that time he was giving lectures on conscience. He had touched on the topic in earlier lectures, but now it was the actual topic of a series.

Naturally he began with a provocative story: A boy steals an apple in the neighbor's garden. Decades later he accuses himself of it as a serious sin.

We laughed, because who of us had not at some time stolen apples or pears?

Abelard said: Isn't it written that you shall not steal?

But to pick an apple in the neighbor's garden, that's not stealing.

What is it? To take other people's property for oneself is theft.

But an apple . . .

An apple, a pear, a silver coin, a gold chain, a horse, where's the limit?

But we know that. An apple isn't a valuable item.

No? Then why did the boy regret this theft so deeply?

He had probably been so strictly brought up that he considered it a sin to steal even one little apple.

He considered it a sin, you say. Who says that it wasn't? If he considered it a sin, then it was a sin. The decisive factor is not the deed, but the intent.

But he didn't have the intent to sin!

But why then did the man that boy had grown up to be regret it? His name was Aurelius Augustinus.

We laughed, but not as openly. I, who had already read the *Confessions*, or rather parts of them, asked, Did he have no other sins to regret?

Abelard looked at me sharply, and only then did he answer, Certainly, he had committed many sins and regretted them.

Yes, I said quietly, he certainly did carry on wildly in his youth.

Abelard didn't dodge the issue. So he did, he said, but did he do so in order to do evil? He did so because he was looking for something that he believed he would find in the realm of concupiscence. He was looking for love, but in the wrong place.

I was stubborn: But when he was young, he didn't know that what he did was bad.

That's just the question, and that's exactly the topic of these lectures. Do people know what is good, what is bad? And if so, how do they come to know it?

[95]

A student said, There are laws that clearly lay down for us what is good, what is bad. Another student said, So we are spoon-fed. We think we are good because we do what the authorities consider good, and people are bad because they don't abide by general laws.

Abelard's counterquestion: Is authority always right, or is there also a subjective conscience?

Here I heard the word "conscience" for the first time. Abelard had never used it. Previously one spoke of the "heart" that had the power of decision.

I asked if the heart and the conscience were one and the same thing.

Abelard said, Conscience comes from the Latin *conscientia*, to know well, and from that is derived consciousness. People have a power within them that they call consciousness. It is the highest judge. This power lives in and with us. It alone is capable of condemning us. For it alone knows the motives for our actions. And the motive alone is what counts. The decisive factor is not the deed, but the motive. Listen to this: A very poor woman had only a single blanket on her bed. It was cold. She wrapped her newborn child in the blanket and held it close to her. In the morning she found the child had suffocated. She was condemned for infanticide. The judge didn't believe her motive. He falsely attributed another motive to her: She wanted to kill the child in an unobtrusive manner. She went to jail, and she regretted her action for the rest of her life. What do you say to that?

We got into a heated discussion. Most were of the opinion that a grievous injustice had been done to the woman. I asked why the woman regretted her action if she really was innocent; even if she didn't want to kill the child, at least not in this manner, it was perhaps all right with her that it died. Perhaps she secretly wished it dead. Would she otherwise have regretted it so much?

Abelard looked at me sharply.

I thought: Now I'll say it, now. Now I'll say: There are mothers for whom their child is a burden, a hindrance, and whom they secretly wish dead because they hadn't wanted it at all, and who send it off to someone else to be taken care of, and have no bad conscience at all because they had a higher motive for doing so.

[96]

I didn't say it. I didn't dare to. Not like that in front of the students. But I thought, You who speak so well about conscience, how is it with your own? Augustine sought nothing but love, the love for God, to be exact, but he didn't find it and became a slave to sensuality and dissipation. And you, Abelard?

Suddenly I was overcome by a great pity for him. Perhaps he had never been loved? His father in a monastery, his mother in a convent, what parents. The child left to his tutor and then sent away to study, alone in the big, cold city. His conscience identical with the (theoretical) morality of the canons: One should suppress one's sexuality; it hinders the high flight of the spirit and, what's more, one's career. Women are to be avoided; they are inferior creatures, nothing but objects of carnal desire, snares for men. So this passionate Breton got to be forty years old and had experienced nothing but knowledge, ambition, controversies.

But there lived in Paris a girl by the name of Heloise. Then the hard crust broke, then the repressed flame leapt up, then what had to happen happened.

Although I was still not certain that my professor was my real father, I felt a great love for him at that moment. I understood: he has never been allowed to live as he wanted. That he was finally robbed of his reproductive organ followed an uncanny logic: he had thought for so long that sexual love was forbidden him, and now, when he loved with body and soul, he was punished for doing the natural, human thing. It wasn't God who punished him; he punished himself. Well, fine, that is his affair; but that he punished not only himself but also Heloise with the inexorable cruelty of an insane love, that is not only his affair, that's also mine, if Heloise really is my birth mother and Abelard's wife and beloved. Am not I likewise castrated, not in body, but in soul? Am I a man? I am healthy; I have my health from my mother. My father, if he is my father, shows susceptibility to all kinds of illnesses and crises.

But what's the point of my health, my strength, my good looks? I carry it all around with me in vain. I can't pass them on to my descendents, because I will never have children, never. By whom would I have them? I can't approach a woman; I'm afraid of hurting women. I have an easy life, a comfortable life

[97]

as a canon, and if I bemoan my fate, then I'm nothing but the circus clown who sweats while hoisting up a beam that, when it falls down, turns out to be as light as a feather.

The heavy, the genuine, beam is borne by Abelard. It is too heavy for one man alone. Now and then he pours out his sorrow to Heloise. I wish he would confide in me. Who except for me could understand him? Who could forgive him? Forgive him in my own name and in that of my mother?

From time to time I loved Abelard and called him "Father" in my heart. From time to time this love broke out of me in a strange way. Once a student said in my presence, He is certainly a great teacher, an innovator, a thinker, but whether what he thinks and teaches will really endure and whether the future of theology belongs to his type of thinking, that is the question. For my taste, he is all too certain, all too sure of himself. As he said recently, he didn't need to prepare himself for his first theological lecture, he relied on his genius; that was already highly arrogant.

I was basically of the same opinion as that student, but I flared up, What do you know about it! This man is a genius, he's the founder of the new theology. He will still be read and quoted when most of his contemporaries have been forgotten and their names can only be found in old lexicons. But he will remain!

My fellow students were stunned. What are you getting so worked up about? How can you rate him like that, overrate him like that?

I screamed (yes, I screamed), You don't understand him. You don't understand that he has introduced a new method of knowing. You don't understand that instead of blind, dead faith he wants the living faith that can prove what it maintains!

Several said, As if faith could be proven. Faith is faith. But your Abelard . . .

My Abelard. If you only knew.

I said, He may be wrong in some things; anyone who dares to take a path that is so new risks making mistakes. But perhaps after a hundred or five hundred years it will turn out that what was considered a mistake is the correct interpretation of a difficult thesis. In the Old Testament the laws were carved in stone tablets. Jesus didn't leave any stone tablets behind. Only

[98]

words. Words that are alive; that stand in dialectical relation to mankind and our evolution. And that is exactly what Abelard wants: to make the faith alive. To free it from the bonds of tradition. People shouldn't believe blindly and brainlessly, but with their reason and their hearts. That is what Abelard wants. . . .

I went on and on. The students listened to me silently. Only gradually did I notice that I had another listener: Abelard had walked in, but went out again without saying anything.

One of the students said, You're becoming a second Abelard, you're getting dangerous.

No, I'm not getting dangerous. I don't have Abelard's strength. I am indeed a rebel, but my rebellion remains internal.

One of the students laughed, but not mockingly, rather jokingly, Look at this Breton here; he hears at Abelard's lectures that not the deed but the intention makes something a sin. And do you not have the intention of attacking church tradition? Even if you never really attack it, you are nonetheless a sinner in your conscience.

The next day Abelard kept me back. He asked: Have you read the *Libri Poenitentiales*?

Yes, I have, but I never understood them.

What didn't you understand?

That they are like a secular law. You have stolen, an ox, you confess and a penance is imposed on you: you have to pay for the ox. If not, then your sin remains. If you pay, it is obliterated. And if you don't confess and no one catches you, you're lucky. The obvious sin is punished, but not the intention. I want to steal an ox, but it gets away from me, no one saw me, I have no sin. When a poor man steals so that his children have something to eat, then that cannot be a sin in God's eyes.

Abelard said, How is it with the words of Christ: When a man looks at a woman and desires her, then he has already committed adultery. How do you understand that?

Not at all, I said.

He laughed briefly and quickly went away.

I was dismayed. Why had he asked me this of all questions that, so it seemed, held no importance for me?

But it became important. Abelard had awakened something in me, whether intentionally or not. In the night after that conversation a pack of wolves attacked me.

Did Abelard look at women? Were they women to him? Temptations? Were there other women in addition to Heloise? Did he think I was a eunuch or a wily swindler or a half holy ascetic? Mustn't a man like Abelard hold me in contempt, me, whose inexperience shows on my face? Is my desire so weak? I contemplated my body, I looked at my penis; it is easily aroused, and when it stretches it is like a young branch, but the skin is fine like silk. What do I do with the thing? Nothing. By God, nothing. I make neither a woman nor myself happy. Useless thing.

Whoever looks at a woman . . . I look at women and girls and feel a fleeting desire, but then the woman suddenly resembles my mother, of whom I have made an image for myself. I have never seen her except in my first year of life; but she is there, and I'm not allowed to embrace her, and therefore I'm not allowed to embrace any other woman, because she could be Heloise, my mother.

My father is a master at torturing himself with self-reproach, almost like Augustine. I don't want to be outdone by him. No, it isn't true, what I just said. I have pushed the image of every other woman away until that of my mother emerged clearly, and then I loved her incestuously. In a fantasy. No, the hint of a fantasy. I have taught myself asceticism.

But now Abelard's preoccupation with the words of Jesus: Whoever looks at a woman and desires her has committed adultery. And if she or the man who desires her isn't married? When one wants to marry a girl, one must look at her and desire her. I don't understand what the Gospel says about that. Can that, mustn't that be a false record of Jesus' words? They do fit in, though, with Abelard's teaching. Not the deed is the sin, but the intention or the thought or the plan, whatever one may call it. But who is master of his thoughts and wishes? And why is it a sin at all to desire a woman? What kind of man sees a beautiful woman and doesn't desire her, doesn't want to sleep with her? Even one's own mother can be desirable. But I don't desire her at all, I desire only a figment of my imagination. Yes, but this figment happens to be my mother, and not just any woman. The Parisian girls are easy to have. I don't want them. It is my mother whom I want. But who is that: my mother?

I wrote these lines months ago. I have something to add to them. Life taught me a lesson. It shamed me. More than that, it pronounced a devastating judgment. I'll be brief: one sunny day I went with some fellow students to the Seine. Whether the game was rigged or not: there were girls waiting there. Five of them. There were six of us. So there was one girl too few. The game began innocently enough. Ballgames, dances, children's games. Then the suggestion to go swimming. Six men, five girls, all naked. At the shore then the sixth girl. She was meant for me. She lured me to her. Then she teased me about my inexperience. That irritated me. I wanted to show her that I was a man. But when I touched her on the breast, a shock went through me. Abelard's hand on my mother's breast. I gathered up my clothes and ran away. Behind me the laughter of the others. When I saw three of them again several hours later, without girls now, I attacked them like a madman. They were so surprised that they didn't defend themselves right away and didn't defend themselves strongly enough. I knocked them to the ground, one after the other. I am strong. At that time I had a wild strength. I could have killed the three of them, but a bailiff drove us apart.

Blood was running down my face. A cut on my forehead. I had to see the doctor. He didn't ask anything; he washed, stitched, and put a bandage on it. He was used to fights. He only said, Come back in three days.

The next night I dream I am a murderer. With the hunting knife in my hand I steal through the Paris streets, accompany a girl into church, to mass, and during Communion I attack her. Her scream wakes me up. I fall asleep and dream again: I see Abelard and Heloise. Far away. On a cloud. They embrace each other. I know they are creating a child. Me. A black angel says to me, You are the child of their sin, you are damned in their place. I scream, and my scream wakes me up. Beside me on a bench is the hunting knife. I hadn't put it there. Who did?

[101]

The next day Abelard looked at me insistently during the lecture. Several times. After the hour he kept me back. In a fight? he said. What was it to him? Fights were quite usual among the students. He held on to me and looked me in the eye. I tore myself loose and ran away. Afterwards I regretted not having said to his face, It was on your account! On your account, and on account of my mother. But would that have been true? And what could he have said to that? It was good that I had said nothing. Good and bad. In any case, I continued carrying the burden alone. Proud of my silent, solitary strength. At least so I thought. I found out later that Abelard knew or suspected much more and suffered. We still hadn't declared ourselves father and son. Once again I wasn't entirely certain that the story was not one of the many Paris rumors that were associated with well-known and famous people. Abelard had many enemies who wanted to drag him through the mud. Through what they considered mud.

When I went back to the doctor on the third day after the fight, he was surprised at how quickly my wound healed.

Good blood, he said.

What good is it, I said.

Why?

I can't pass it on.

What do you mean by that?

What I say.

What kind of nonsense are you talking?

You don't understand me? Or do you? I never want to have a child. My own calamity is quite enough. I don't want to create a destiny.

Do you want to become a monk?

No, not that either. Not a monk, not a priest, not a father. I will become what I am: the shadow in the shadow of my father.

The doctor attended to my bandage silently.

When I was leaving he said, It's a pity about you.

How that remark hit me! It's a pity about Abelard, the doctor in Corbeil had said. It's a pity about Abelard; he was born too early.

It's a pity about Astrolabe, I said as I went out, it's a pity about him. If only he hadn't been born.

When I sat in front of Abelard again the next day, the blood suddenly rose to my head. I summoned all my strength and wished him dead. I wished him dead with such vehemence that he broke off in mid-sentence and lost his train of thought. That had never happened to him before; he always spoke freely and easily, didn't repeat himself, made no slips of the tongue; it was as if he were reading from a manuscript, but no page lay in front of him, and what he said always seemed to be the idea of the moment. But the idea that seemed to have just come to him was the fruit of much thinking. Idea after idea yielded a free-floating but clear system. That was exciting and fascinating. It was no surprise that there were great minds among his students: Guido di Castello (later Pope Celestine II), Otto von Freising, the uncle of Frederick Barbarossa, Roland Bandinelli (later Pope Alexander III), and others; some later became cardinals. We young students were amazed and learned how to debate. No more dry parroting of prescribed texts. A free spirit reigned, but it was this very spirit that taught us the problem of freedom: it wasn't enough that we lived according to prescribed moral laws, we had to take the burden of our own conscience upon us. That was Abelard's great new idea: You are your own lawmaker and judge.

That means: know the motives for your own actions. "Know thyself." Abelard often quoted the Delphic word. To know oneself meant, according to Abelard, to ask oneself why and for what one did something. It meant delving into one's own depths. But it also meant not condemning everything that ecclesiastical ascetics called bad.

At the time, I made note of several sentences from the lectures of that semester. Sentences that seem highly contradictory to me now that I have read Abelard's *Story of My Misfortunes*. The knot can't be untied even with clever dialectics. At least I am incapable of it.

At the time I also noted (and was not mistaken, because I found this sentence again later in his *Ethics*):

[103]

When a person performs a deed, it can be called good or bad. The verdict depends on different factors: on the time in which the deed took place, on the intention that was pursued, and on the mindset from which it sprang.

At that time I wrote in the margin: "Mindset, as I understand it, means the whole moral character of the person performing the deed." I don't know if Abelard would have been in agreement with this sentence. For certain his understanding of morality was other than the current theology.

Abelard's teaching received its impetus from his condemnation of the dissolute life in the monasteries and among clerics, the secularization of the church, the accumulation of wealth in the church, the mechanical saying of prayers, the empty cultic rituals that were more a magical, pagan invocation of spirits than a talk with God, and above all the superficiality of religious belief. Abelard once said: "People drone out the Credo and don't know what they're saying; if questioned rigorously, hardly anyone would know what he really believes." So too regarding morality (he said this another time, in a smaller circle):

A man thinks he is virtuous because he obeys all that the law dictates and doesn't do anything that is forbidden by the church, but he is still far removed from genuine Christianity, which requires much more of a person, namely, the free decision of his own conscience. Therein lies man's dignity, that he is free in his way of thinking. For that purpose, God gave him a conscience.

The church authority would naturally have to understand this sentence as heresy, because no one but the church has the right to say what is good, what is bad. It alone is the highest moral instance. Where would we be if everyone made up his own morality?

I of course believe that the personal conscience is a much stricter lawmaker and judge than any external authority.

In this I am entirely Abelard's pupil, just as you, Heloise, are his pupil. We both ate from the tree of knowledge, and our knowledge is dialectical. Is it not your own particular sort of Abelard's dialectics that you can write you feel simultaneously innocent and guilty? If you feel both guilty and innocent, wherein lies the guilt? May I say it to your face? Your guilt was your immoderation. You gave yourself up, yourself, your person, you submitted blindly to the man, you let him force you, indeed, beat you into having sexual intercourse with him. You became his slave. Out of love, yes, certainly, but you should have put him, the man, in his place. You only encouraged his own immoderation. You put him on a throne. You made him God. You wrote yourself, you were "always more afraid of displeasing Abelard than God." You put Abelard in the place of God. This man became your God. Don't say you loved the divine part in him. No, don't say that. You don't say it, either. You simply loved this handsome, enigmatic man with elemental force. Everything else existed only as a shadow for you. Abelard alone was real. You worshipped a strange God. In doing so, you forgot the true God. No, not forgot: accused him, cursed him. Abelard reproaches you for that many times in his letters, saying that once you are in the convent you are only allowed to have one single beloved. Easily said. How can a passionate girl, having become acquainted with physical love and desire, love an invisible bridegroom, an untouchable God? In one of his letters Abelard writes that Heloise should think of the suffering of Christ on the cross in order to consider her own suffering slight.

That is the talk of someone who has forcibly been made an ascetic. That cannot help a passionate young woman at all. It can more likely become the blasphemous question: Why did you die, Christ? So that I, Heloise, suffer unredeemed, damned to a life in the convent? Abelard demanded that she humbly obey and atone for her sin. But confound it all: What sin does he, setting himself up as judge, attribute to her? That she gave herself to him when he, the handsome, famous, fierce man courted her so passionately? Was she supposed to refuse him? That would have been a sin against life and love. Was what they experienced, these two, not something beautiful? And I don't understand why Abelard in his *Story of My Misfortunes* speaks of the "filth" in which they both wallowed. What is filthy about it? I admit that it disgusts me when whores offer themselves to me and show me their breasts and private parts and sell themselves. But Heloise was no whore; she was a pure girl, like a bride. Whatever the two of them did, it happened out of love.

[105]

But Abelard wrote in his *Story of My Misfortunes*: "God's grace has delivered me from these despicable organs." Despicable organs? Weren't they created by God? Can something be despicable that serves life? And not only for reproduction, no, also for enjoyment of love. Does God create something for the ruin of man? Is it a test? Was Abelard tried like Job to see if he was really true, namely, chaste? What kind of God is that who gave man those organs for pleasure and then punished him when he used them? Naturally, I would never have dared to say this sentence openly. But Abelard, he dared. In a lecture he said, Did God create apples so that people wouldn't be allowed to eat them and will be severely punished for it, even if they do so in the firm belief that the apples were created by God for the nourishment and pleasure of man?

I later read in another place in Abelard's *Story of My Misfortunes* that he experienced the castration as God's punishment. What logic: the same Abelard condemns Origen, who castrated himself in order not to be plagued by his sex. What doesn't suit Abelard about that? That Origen acted on his own authority. But is his deed not greater than Abelard's simple passive suffering of the castration? Wherein lies the difference? Abelard's suffering was punishment and grace simultaneously, both from the hand of God. According to the will of God. Says Abelard. What a God. Every time Abelard speaks in his lectures about the will of God, I feel the intense desire to leap up and shout, So it wasn't your passion that put me in the world, it was the will of God, and if it was the will of God, then it was also his will that you two slept together in red-hot passion; so what is sin and who has sinned, if everything is the will of God? Abelard, your philosophy that seems so clear has some dim and nasty corners. Where you think you have to comply fully with the requirement of total abstinence in order to atone for all your "sins" is precisely where you get into a contradiction with yourself and your theology of sin. Was it your intent to sin? You had no intent at all, neither good nor bad; you were ambushed by the powerful god Eros and saw no reason to resist him when he offered you the most beautiful thing in life: the great love.

But perhaps you have never really loved. Perhaps what Heloise once complained about is true: you only "took" her. But no, no: you loved her. Only why did you never fully stand by this love, by the past? Why do you call filth what was so beautiful? Oh, your exaggerated ideal of chastity. You have read too much Paul and Jerome. You have made an ideal of perfection for yourself. You alone are the best, the first. You with your diabolical arrogance. If God punishes you, then perhaps it is for one thing alone, that you have confined my young mother in your net of guilt feelings, penitence, and asceticism and also wanted to rob her of the one thing that remained hers in life: the memory, as sweet as it is bitter, of the time when you were lovers. I fear you begrudged her that she was still capable of physical love, even if she didn't give herself to a man. She should be "castrated" in her way. That's why she had to enter the convent before you entered the monastery!

And that was supposed to be the will of God? You pretended your will of man was the will of God. Can it be the will of a good God to lock up a girl for life in a convent, because she has loved consummately? What a God. Either he is a jealous father, or he is blind like the classical Moira, or God is the Christian transformation of Chronos, who eats his own children.

Dearest Mother, how can I help you? Does it help you if I hate the one who makes you suffer so much? If I someday publicly charge Abelard with spiritual murder?

Oh, I am certain you would defend him, because by defending him you defend your love and your fate. You obeyed Abelard, your fate, "voluntarily."

But the question of guilt comes up again and again. If, according to Abelard, sin is only what happens with full insight into its sinfulness and with complete freedom of will, then he and Heloise are innocent.

"I am guilty, and yet also entirely innocent," writes Heloise. According to her own conscience, she is innocent. But Abelard, tormenting himself and her mercilessly, wants to persuade her that she is partly to blame along with him. Thus he continues to poison Heloise's difficult monastic peace, and in one of her letters to Abelard, the professional theologian and spiritual advisor to the nuns, she puts two questions to him.

"Is one guilty when one carries out an order from one's own master?" (On first reading, I read "heart" instead of "master.")[2] The other question: "If

2. The German words *Herr* (master) and *Herz* (heart) are similar.

someone forces someone else to do something bad together with him, is the consent of the other then a sin?"

Was what Abelard wanted something bad? Did he really force Heloise? From time to time she struggled against having sexual relations. I can imagine that this insatiable, violent man was too much for the girl; tiresome too. But his orders were orders. She obeyed. She yielded because she loved him.

Perhaps if they had really lived their marriage, even for a few years, this first flame would have gone out and the marriage would have become an everyday burden.

Perhaps, if one believes in an interfering God, this was the grace that he showed the two of them: that the radiance of their first love would not fade. Their suffering kept their love young and intense; they suffered for the rest of their lives. But they suffered differently. Heloise suffered and suffers from unfulfilled longing and from her "voluntary" incarceration. That is human suffering. One finds it moving.

Abelard, however, suffered from arrogance. He suffered because he didn't live up to his ideal of perfection. How often he speaks of the "dirt he wallowed in with Heloise." What he did not forgive himself was his betrayal of the ideal: I, Abelard, the great, the unique, I became a common sexual being. What a fall from the throne.

Yet after a while no one was concerned about his past. Presumably his "affair" made him even more liked among the students. Later he was so brilliant that people forgot about it. But Abelard never forgot and never forgave himself his past. Though I have the suspicion that he didn't regret a sin, rather that he did not forgive himself for having become an ordinary man, man in all his weakness. That shouldn't have been allowed to happen to him, Abelard. He was ashamed. But shame isn't regret.

Heloise never regretted, not even on Abelard's orders. In this, she finally dared disobedience and revolt. And the revolt went through all authorities to the highest judge, against whom she blasphemed. She was never a hypocrite. Hardly had a word that revealed something like regret escaped her than she took it back, on Abelard's orders. Again and again she emphasizes that what she experienced was beautiful and great – bitter but also sweet – and that this feeling has remained. She never forgot the embraces; even years later she longed physically for his embrace and suffered from the imposed deprivation. She curses God until Abelard instructs her to be silent. And she is silent from then on. Not another word about it in her letters. Obedient even in them. But let there be no mistake about it: this silence was no act of submission, rather an act of wonderfully defiant arrogance: I am silent, but don't think that I am crawling, broken, to the cross; my hereafter unspoken no to my fate is a silent scandal, for you too, Abelard.

There are letters for the sake of which I could beat Abelard. As when he writes for her consolation:

It would be an execrable loss if you, abandoned to carnal desire, were to bear with pain several children for the world, whereas you now bear with jubilation a great number for heaven. In the world you would only be a woman, now you even stand over men and have turned Eve's curse into Mary's blessing. These holy hands that are now allowed even to open the books of the Scriptures would have to do, in the world, the lowest work of a wife.

Prattle. Whether Heloise welcomed new novices with jubilation is a question. Perhaps it gave her proud satisfaction that her convent community steadily expanded. But the exaggeration: Eve's curse turned into Mary's blessing by Heloise. Abelard, all your wonderful rhetoric doesn't help Heloise. She knows as your pupil – or she knew even before that – that only the intention counts. Did Heloise ever have the intention of becoming a sort of redeeming Mary? She never accepted this role that you forced on her. Perhaps it was for your consolation that you, the jailer, put a crown on her head. But Heloise didn't want a crown. She was so realistic that she didn't even hope for a reward from God for the sacrifice of her life. Nothing. Abelard had been taken from her and with him everything, even God. She can't lie and be hypocritical and deceive herself. A different nun in her situation would perhaps, infected by Abelard's exaggeration, have put up with this "canonization while still alive" and would have regarded herself as richly rewarded in the certainty of her reward in eternity. Heloise couldn't care less about holiness and a reward in heaven. She wants to live. She can't be swayed by lies. She wants Abelard.

[109]

She hates God, who enticed him away from her. If it was him. If. If it wasn't just Abelard's defiant pride. And if his ascetic life wasn't just the consequence of the castration. Or his immoderate ambition not only to be a great ascetic himself, but also to induce Heloise to do the same. Heloise has her own idea of life. She lost Abelard and as a poor substitute for him received the office of superior of the order. She performs her duties outstandingly. That is another matter. It is her quite worldly ambition to run her convent in the best way possible. In an exemplary fashion. As to how she is doing, whose concern is that? He whose concern it is and to whom she complains (he is after all her husband and the father of her son) answers her cries for love with pious sermons. Of what help to Heloise in her situation is a sermon that might have moved others to tears. For Heloise it is empty talk, of that I'm sure.

Aren't you moved to tears when you behold the Son of God on the cross? He is innocent and for your sake, for the sake of all people, he was beaten, crowned with thorns, hung on the cross between thieves. . . . Dear Sister, keep him always before your eyes, your true bridegroom, the bridegroom of the entire church, who allowed himself to be crucified for you. And how he carries his cross.

Did Christ really die for such sins as Heloise committed out of pure, strong love for a man? He didn't die for the sake of the natural "sin of the flesh," and certainly not for the sake of those loving embraces. He died for the hordes of hypocrites, cruel rulers, masters who beat their servants, priests and monks who accumulate money, underhanded slanderers, perhaps also for such diabolical minds as Abelard's was, although he apparently converted by doing what he advised Heloise to do: meditate on the sufferings of Christ. But Heloise, the girl who gave herself to the one single man in unconditional love – no, this sin is no cause for the death of Christ. Didn't Abelard, who knows his Bible, forget the words of Christ to the adulteress? The people he condemned were the male hypocrites. For the women he found other words. He told them how they could save themselves from downfall through repentance. "You daughters of Jerusalem, weep for yourselves and your children."

Your children. When Abelard read that sentence, did he think of his own child? Certainly not. Or did he? Isn't it an outrageous affront to Heloise when he gives her the Gospel text to consider: "The time will come when people will say: Blessed are the infertile and the bodies that have not given birth, and the breasts that have not suckled." What a defamation of life. What a desperate, evil attempt to damn his own past, to wish away his own wife and his own child!

And that is supposed to be a letter of consolation to a woman whose heart has been broken? Certainly, he is also writing these epistolary sermons to console himself. By raising Heloise to the Queen of Sorrows he is accusing himself. Once he even clearly calls himself her seducer.

But then comes another of those sentences in *The Story of My Misfortunes* for which I hate my father:

God sees a guilty pair and punishes only the man. In that respect, God's mercy makes allowances for the weakness of a woman. As a sexual being you were allowed to be weaker than the man, as an individual you were stronger in your self-control. So God's lenient lovingkindness was well deserved because you weren't as punishable as I. . . .

O Abelard, you egoist even in self-accusation. You feel your punishment was heavy. And Heloise? Less guilty, less punished. Haven't you grasped that her punishment was jail for life and the sacrifice of her youth and femininity? That you were castrated seems to you the worst possible punishment. Wasn't everything taken from Heloise that was her life? Even in suffering you want to be the greater one. That reminds me of Paul: "I have worked more and suffered more than all of you. . . ." I'm ashamed to be a man because men are like that. I understand. I'm a man, but one whose soul is castrated. That's why I understand women, even if they are a forbidden fruit to me. Or perhaps precisely because they are.

How the sentence strikes me that I found in one of your letters, Mother, years, many years later:

Would to God that my sick heart were as willing to obey as is my hand when I write. I want to forbid my hand to write what I could not forbid my mouth to say.

So they didn't see each other or speak to each other for years? They exchange letters. To be precise, Heloise forces him to write by putting matter-of-fact questions to the spiritual advisor.

In one of the letters she complains bitterly that he isn't fulfilling his duty to look after the Convent of the Paraclete. Oh, Heloise, Mother, no matter how good a prioress you were, you still always remain Abelard's lover and wife. You base your exhortation of Abelard on a word that he himself quotes in his *Story of My Misfortunes*. It's a sentence from an encyclical from Pope Leo IX. "We clearly declare that no bishop, elder, deacon, or subdeacon may take his religious duties as a pretext for removing himself from his obligation to ensure the welfare of his wife; he must provide her with food and clothing."

I have to laugh aloud: Heloise had once refused to marry him because caring for his family would interfere with his higher duties. Now he has to care not for a small family, but for a group of nuns. And that very woman who feared that Abelard as a husband and father would lose too much time on his family now complains that he hardly ever takes the time to come to the Paraclete. She never asks him to visit her, she only asks him to come to see that everything is in order. Oh, poor Mother Heloise, all your letters of concern about your nuns have a palimpsest that is clearly legible through your letters. It reads: Beloved, still and always beloved, I long for you; come!

He came. Seldom enough. But he did come. And then there were secret embraces in the half-light of the church. Fleeting probably, but embraces nonetheless. Abelard's claim to asceticism wasn't so strong that the sight of his beautiful, young, passionate lover and wife left him cold.

How absurd that people aren't permitted to live their love.

It was under the cloak of necessity that Abelard ran into temptation's arms: he had to look after the convent. There were people in the vicinity of the convent who held it against Abelard that he took so little care of the Paraclete, saying it showed a lack of responsibility. Wasn't he the official advisor, the preacher, the father confessor? So he went there "purely out of brotherly love," as he wrote. He didn't go there often, but often enough to arouse slanderous gossip: Look how he still longs for the woman, even after becoming a monk and a priest; he can't manage to live without his mistress;

he can't stand to be away from his former lover. Of course after his castration it won't be as it once was, but . . .

Abelard writes about that in his *Story of My Misfortunes*:

My bodily loss usually takes away any suspicion that it could even come to such a sin. That is precisely the reason why eunuchs are chosen when women are to be held in safekeeping.

Don't make me laugh. As inexperienced as I am, I would know what I could do with a woman if I were a eunuch. After all, there's more than just one way of showing love and affection. I hope that Abelard and Heloise also know such games. A wicked thought: I would be a good lover for Heloise.

Abelard, in his *Story of My Misfortunes*, justifies his visits in the Paraclete in his theological way: he quotes all the relationships between holy men and women that were "pure" and still aroused suspicion: Christ and the women; all the women in the apostles' entourage; prophets are often widows' guests; the church fathers who headed convents; Jesus Christ, who entrusts his mother to a young man; St. Jerome and his female friend Paula. And so on. Does he need the justification? He quotes St. Augustine: "He who relies on his good conscience and does not take into consideration his reputation in the eyes of others is cruel. There are two things: a good conscience and a good reputation. A good conscience is for you; your good reputation is for your neighbors."

When I read these sentences, I thought, What a good reputation I had as a student, and I have it still as a good canon, but how is it with my conscience? I, who in my dreams rape my mother and murder my father. . . . I always carried my hunting knife with me: wasn't it with intent to murder? Who suspected that? Abelard? He looked at me so often during his lectures, and his gaze was sometimes full of mistrust, even fear, and then again full of a feeling that, as I now know, was close to opening the floodgates.

I don't know whether I hated him or loved him. Both. Not as if sometimes hate dominated, sometimes love. It was both simultaneously, or something else, a third thing, something that cut my heart in two and didn't let me be young.

At that time I resumed my rides to the Paraclete. I didn't knock at the gate anymore. I was no beggar. I was an accuser, Heloise. I accuse you of the immoderateness of your love. I accuse you of violating your own person. I accuse you of having raised Abelard to be your God.

I wasn't only an accuser, I was also a defender: You have loved, you stood bravely and unconditionally, you knew how close together Eros and Thanatos are, your love is as strong as death, you sinner will become the model of true love. Your love washes away everything that Abelard calls "filth." Abelard is accused, not Heloise.

And yet, you are an accomplice, Mother. You shouldn't have submitted blindly to this man. You shouldn't have strengthened his immoderateness even more. You shouldn't have deified him. You shouldn't have elevated him to a throne to which no mortal is entitled. "I have always been more afraid of displeasing Abelard than God."

The defender (who is leaning against the hard, silent convent wall behind which you live, Mother) says, But what can an invisible God be for a passionate girl? This invisible one, can she love him? She loves the visible and tangible one, the man of flesh and blood. She loves life. Life!

I feel the rough wall against my back. I stroke it. I scratch out moss and stones. The wall resists. My fingers bleed. I scrape my forehead bloody on this wall. Who built such walls, who invented such prisons, who had the courage to lock up young women for life? Who has the authority to separate lovers and to damn love? Who condemns men to celibacy? What kind of church is that? Or, what kind of God is that? What sense is there in saying no to life, which after all is given to us for our joy and pleasure?

Scratching senselessly at the wall like that, more an animal than a human being, I get the suspicion: this God is jealous. Doesn't it say that in the Bible? A jealous God, who wants the love of mankind for himself alone and punishes anyone who loves one of his creatures more than him?

You jealous one! I scream, You are no God, you are a demon, who hates love and declares it a sin and punishes it severely. A God to whom renunciation of life, of love, of lust, of children is pleasing. That cannot be. You are a God of the living, not of the dead. It is nothing but the will of the church that compels all the forces of life to serve it in order to strengthen its worldly or its magical power. I hate this church. Why does Abelard remain in it? He has experienced enough harm from it. Abelard, fetch your beloved out of this prison, out of this tomb, call her to life, to love!

"Girl, arise!" said Christ to the dead child. And she stood up and lived.

If Abelard said that, would Heloise emerge from the convent tomb? An idle thought; he won't say that. His mouth remains closed, the tomb remains closed.

What am I against them? A nothing. I have always complied. A sheep that should be happy to have found a fold and a shepherd.

Come, Astrolabe, son of my friend Heloise, whom I silently love; come, you can become a canon in my province, said Peter the Venerable.

This too is a fold. Here too a gate was shut. Forever. I am a good canon. No one sees the hunting knife in my pocket.

I should have refused the offer. Should have gone away. Better a poor free forester than a fat canon, tolerated in the church for his parents' sake.

Don't I come from a good long line of knights? Mustn't my parents be ashamed of me? Mustn't they think, Is this son really our flesh and blood? Have we with all our passion brought nothing better into the world? Does Abelard not want to recognize me because I am a strange nothing to him?

That summer I tormented myself so terribly that several times I wished for death and was close to killing myself.

Roger saw my suffering. He asked me to accompany him on a trip south.

What should I do in the south? Suddenly I felt the desire to ride to Brittany. Without Roger. Away from the ceaseless bustle at the university. Away from these talkative, malicious city folk, away from having to think. And away from this Abelard with his uncannily searching look. Away. I wasn't sick, hadn't had a breakdown like Abelard when he fled from Corbeil. And yet I was also in flight. Why didn't I kill Abelard? . . .

Paris drew me back. But I resisted the pull. I rode on. I left Corbeil behind me. I took the way that I had come two years before in the opposite direction, an ignorant boy then, curious about Paris, comparatively happy, even if unsettled by my foreboding of a twist of fate.

From a distance I saw the walls of the Paraclete. Onward, onward. How I had hurried my horse and my groom on the ride to Paris. Now I rode alone and slowly, as if I had no goal. I stopped here and there, stayed overnight in inexpensive inns, talked with the farmers, and was glad when I heard my native dialect, a rough way of speaking, in which one can't tell lies as in smooth Parisian.

It was July. In Paris the air was boiling in the narrow streets. Here on the plateau a fresh northwest wind was blowing. Pure air, free of ghosts.

The little oak forest that marked the southeast boundary of the Pallet estates. I dismounted. The first steps on my native soil. The first living things I met: one of our large flocks of sheep. A ram butted me; I had to laugh, I took him by the horns and he calmed down, he knew his master's grip. The shepherd no longer recognized me. But the dogs, the three shaggy, white sheepdogs, they recognized me. They leapt up on me and licked my face and hands. For them I was their old playmate. I let the horse roam around freely. The dogs came and went. I lay on my back and was happy. A feeling I hadn't experienced for a long time: peace. At home. In the midst of genuine realities: dogs, sheep, pasture land, blackthorn hedges, oaks, clouds, and wind, and earth, a lot of earth, tangible. What came first: grass or the idea of grass? Ridiculous problems, artificial, crazy. What is important is what exists for humans, was created for them. I was so happy that I rolled around in the grass and shouted with joy. The dogs came running, sprang over me, romped beside me. Happiness. That's what it is. Philosophy and theology: nothing but demoniacal pride and vain pains to know what one can only know when one grasps it with the senses and loves it. That's what it was: to love!

Abelard, come back, come home! I called, come with your Heloise, you will be happy here.

Evening came, and finally I had to enter the house. Why was I afraid to do so? I brought in my horse and tied it to the beam in front of the stall. A woman appeared: Denise. She was carrying a basket full of early apples; I recognized their tart smell. I stood still; she had already seen me. She let the basket fall. Neither of us was prepared for this reunion. So it happened that I called, "Mother!" Denise embraced me and wept.

[116]

Suddenly she pushed me away, wouldn't have me carry the apple basket, and said briefly, God bless your arrival.

She didn't say: your return. It was clear to her that I had only come for a short time, and she didn't take it at face value when I said, Now I want to stay here forever.

No, she said, you don't want that. You belong there, where . . .

She interrupted herself. She took refuge in practical things: Your room is unchanged, the maids will clean it quickly. We'll be alone this evening; the men are at a tournament.

I sensed that she was somewhat embarrassed to be alone with me, and I too felt awkward. She escaped into the kitchen to prepare an evening meal for me, and I tended to my horse. The evening remained light a long time. I walked through the apple orchard and looked at the cows that were grazing nearby. Peace. Why not stay here? Why study? I wouldn't shine in the academic world. How do I actually see my future? I don't see it at all. Everything lies in darkness; even Abelard and Heloise disappear in the mist. Let them live their suffering. I'm me. I want to live my own life. I don't need parents.

I say "Mother" to Denise, who brings me my dinner, she, not one of the maids, and she says quietly, My little one.

She adds, Don't say "Mother" anymore. I'm not entitled to the name. You know how it is. I'm your aunt.

Come on now: aunt. Who brought me up for eighteen years? Who? You didn't give birth to me, I know that, but you were my mother to me. You taught me to speak, and your language is mine. You put me to bed and sang your Breton songs for me. You gave me affection. You praised me when I gave our tutor good answers. You punished me, remember, when I tied clattering sticks to a cow's tail and when I lied, saying it wasn't I who had done it. You told me what is good and what is bad. It was you who gave me confidence in life.

But, she said, you don't have it any more. You feel betrayed by us, your foster parents, and betrayed by your natural parents. You have neither parents nor foster parents anymore. You feel abandoned. You are full of grief and wrath.

Yes, that I am. You don't know that I am a murderer, in thought, in wishes.

Don't say such big, wicked words. You are good. It's just that life has imposed a twisted, hard fate on you. But eat and drink now. I have to help the maids. We'll talk afterward, if you want.

I ate and drank. How good the rough rye bread tasted with the ham and malt beer. Home. The rough table too. The smoky air too. Everything genuine. Everything exactly what it is. Why not stay here. Marry one of the pretty girls. Have children. Hunt wild boar. Take part in tournaments. Breed horses. Why all the studying. Why Paris. If Abelard had stayed here . . .

I fell asleep with my head on the tabletop. Denise woke me gently.

Now we'll talk, she said.

Why did the two of you never tell me who my natural parents are?

Why? Because they wanted it that way. You were supposed to be a carefree, happy child. That's why they brought you here.

When did they bring me here?

Twenty years ago. They came one night, both on horseback. I recognized Abelard, but not the woman who came with him. She wore a nun's habit.

So I'm the child of a nun after all.

No. Wait a minute. She was only wearing a nun's robe, but she wasn't a nun. She wasn't supposed to be recognized.

Why not?

Because everything had to be kept secret.

But all Paris knew the story of their affair. The professor had become a minstrel. He wrote poetry and composed, and people sang his songs in the streets and taverns. Secret, secret – I have to laugh. Abelard didn't have the courage to stand by his love.

Yes, he did, he stood by it. He stood by it so much that he married Heloise, although she didn't want to. Yes, she was the one who didn't want to get married, because Abelard's career might have been destroyed by this marriage. She was, oh, my little one, she was and is a great woman. What am I in comparison to her.

You would never have abandoned and disowned me, Denise. Don't talk to me of greatness. It's a sin to abandon a child.

You shouldn't judge. She's your mother. . . .

[118]

Do stop, Denise, she's not my mother, she was and is just Abelard's lover. I'm nothing to her, nothing. A troublesome little bundle that one lays aside. Here, Denise, you take the brat, bring him up, I have more important things to do.

Oh, my little one, how hard you are. What do you know of fate and how it weaves and binds. You didn't see how your mother cried when she rode away from here without you.

And then Denise did the only proper thing: she put her arm around me and let me cry. Between my sobs, with my head nestled on her shoulder, I unburdened my mind. She sat still like a figure of the Madonna. She let me talk and cry and curse. When I became calmer, she asked the unexpected question, How did you find out who your father is? And does he know that you know?

We both know it, but we are scared stiff to say so to each other and to show it. So we play a strange game. Denise, for two years I've been his student at the university; he is my philosophy teacher. We see each other every day. I've already taken four exams from him. And done well. And all the while we stared at each other. Once he beat around the bush and mentioned Berengar and asked if I came from Brittany. But that was all. Too little and already too much. Denise, I hate him!

Oh, my little one, what a thing to say.

But that's the way it is: I hate him. He seduced a girl, got her pregnant, drove her into a convent. He knocked her up, then cast off and disowned the child.

That's not true. He often sent secret messengers to ask how you were, and he sent money.

Stop, stop. He sent money. And thought that washed away all his guilt.

We saved the money. It's a large sum. We sent you the money for your studies out of that. We couldn't have afforded it.

To hell with this money. I want nothing more to do with it. I'd rather go begging than take more money from him. Denise, I don't want to study anymore. I want to stay with the two of you. You are good, you're my parents.

[119]

You say that now. You're already much too far removed from our simple way of life. You're already Abelard's student. You have to think. We have no time for such thinking. We are pious people. We believe and pray and work.

Damned thinking, damned theology. Where does it lead to? They are right, those people who denounce Abelard as a heretic.

No, said Denise and was suddenly harsh and had Abelard's hard face. No, they aren't right. He isn't a heretic. He was always devout. But he was always a thinker too, even as a child he always wanted to know everything very exactly. And what he wants now is for people to be allowed to think about what they should believe. Why would a God have given us the ability to think if we aren't allowed to use it?

Denise, you are intelligent, Abelard's sister. You are right. He became a thinker out of love for the truth, not out of the spirit of contradiction. Abelard's belief is alive, and whoever listens to him understands his great intention.

Denise listened to me attentively and perplexed.

You're defending him! How can you say that you hate him and would like to kill him!

If only he weren't my father.

Why aren't you proud to have him as your father?

Denise, you don't have to try to teach me filial love. You yourself know that Abelard is no father and that one can admire him but also has to fear him.

You yourself aren't certain whether you should defend him or condemn him.

I think you see through him and just don't want me to see through him too. According to your morality, people should honor and love their fathers. I know. But Abelard taught me to think. So I think, and I also think about him. He's a genius, that's clear. I know that one can't compare him with ordinary people. But I'm not blind to his faults. He's arrogant, quarrelsome, dictatorial, and not just when it's a matter of scholarship and truth. He is haughty by nature and his ambition is immoderate.

Is it his fault that he is the way he is?

[120]

Who's talking about fault? I'm painting a picture of him.

So you think. But don't forget that he is also immoderate in good things: in courage, in his love of truth, and in love and loyalty. A knight from the Berengar family, a man of passion, a famous, venerated scholar, and then a monk, and all that in a single person. Who can endure that?

All right. We can go on and on about him. We can't grasp him verbally. He's like this and this and this, he's many things, he's great and small. Someone like him is difficult to tolerate. There's only one person who could and can do it: Heloise. Because she was and is greater than he is.

Well, look who's talking. When was the last time you saw her?

Saw her. I've never seen her. She doesn't want to see me. She has me turned away at the convent gate.

Don't you understand that? Being a natural mother doesn't count. Animals are mothers too. Being a spiritual mother is what counts. She's the mother of many daughters, she's a nun, she's the prioress or even the abbess. In any case, she's just as radical as Abelard. All or nothing.

I have my doubts, Denise. But now I'm tired.

We went to bed. But I didn't sleep.

I slept seventeen years of my life in this room, a deep, healthy sleep usually; not always, because sex was on my mind, and my desires ran downstairs to the pretty, healthy, well-rounded maids, but order reigned in this house. So I had to learn self-control. But why? What did I gain from it? Did Abelard grow up that way too? Until the dam broke. That's how I came into being: the child of pent-up passion.

What had Denise said? Heloise had been as radical as Abelard. All or nothing. I had my doubts.

That night in Pallet I knew neither Abelard's *Story of My Misfortunes* nor your correspondence. I knew nothing or only vaguely about your suffering, Heloise. I didn't know that you didn't enter the convent voluntarily. Not out of love for God, but because Abelard demanded it of you. All or nothing, yes, but in your love for Abelard. You would have died for him if he had asked you to. Jephthah's daughter. That was simpler and her death was quicker. What did Denise say? The two of them were equally radical. Nevertheless,

[121]

Abelard accuses himself of having engaged in all kinds of love games with you in the darkest corner of the refectory. All or nothing. No, not all, and also not nothing. Oh, you two. Should I hate you, detest you, pity you?

That night in my old room pity predominated. But toward morning it was clear to me that it was self-pity. There was something else besides: I was Abelard's pupil, to be sure, and I had learned to think instead of believing blindly, but even so I had believed blindly. There was always a remnant of childlike belief in me. I never surrendered myself to Abelard's way of believing, this way of laying a solid foundation for the faith, a foundation that was constructed out of doubts. I wanted to remain a child. To stay here. To have security. Abelard likewise wanted security, but he fought for a new, hard security. He wanted a belief that was hope, not certainty; a security of insecurity.

Suddenly I longed for Abelard. Not for a father, but for the teacher, the only great one, as it seemed to me. I had to go back to Paris. Several weeks of holiday here, no more, no longer. If I stayed longer, it could be that I would put down roots in my native soil. How much simpler life would be for me here. Wasn't this studying in Paris a trap of the devil?

The next day we got to talking about Abelard again.

Tell me about him, Denise.

What should I tell. Even as a child he was himself. He always knew everything better than others, and he really did; He was so clever that it frightened our parents, as if he had made a pact with the devil. He was obstinate, uncompromising, quarrelsome, but also always magnanimous, he gave everything away, with a light heart, but he was never happy and never a child. He wasn't disobedient, it didn't come to that; he did what he wanted, and people let him have his way, they even accepted his fits of anger. He could get terribly wild when he caught someone telling a lie. He never lied.

Did he love his parents?

That wasn't an issue with us. Your grandparents were strict, taciturn people. There were no caresses, and one didn't show love. And both of them entered the cloisters and left us behind. That's just the way it is. We didn't expect and demand more than they gave us.

But you knew your parents. You weren't abandoned and disowned as children.

But we didn't have famous parents, my little one. We had no reputation to defend, because it didn't occur to anyone to damage it.

I envy you. The two of you live the right way here. Whoever starts to think, to think the way Abelard does, places himself in mortal danger. Perhaps thinking is a sin. I should stay here, in quiet obedience.

My little one, you can't do that. It's too late. There's no going back for you.

And what lies ahead of me, Denise? You see, now you are silent, because you know as well as I do that I am nothing in comparison to my parents. But tell me: what do you think of Heloise?

She was so young and so inexperienced, and Abelard was her first love. How should she not love him. That was the kind of love that one can't control. The fire burns. No water can extinguish it.

Well, fine. I can understand that she, the young woman, the girl, was burning with passion. But tell me something about her. After all, I was born in this house.

How brave she was during your birth. She had strong labor pains; she was so slender that we had to fear for her life and for yours. Not one scream crossed her lips. But when you were finally born, she laughed and cried and was beside herself with joy.

But, Mother Denise, you were otherwise always so strict about morality. How are you talking now?

Morality, morality, that's one word, passion is another, and love is yet another. My God, how they loved each other. How blissfully happy the young woman was with her child.

Oh yes. And then she gave it to you and rode away, bliss and child forgotten. She had no use for a child; it would bother her when she was studying and disrupt the career of her beloved. What does a child count when it's the child of people with boundless ambition?

Oh, my little one, that's all so confused I can't unravel it. I only know that you'll go away again and that I'll lose you.

What are you saying? You are and will remain my . . .

[123]

Be quiet. I'm not your mother. I don't want to be what I'm not.

Those words rang in my ears and remained in my heart. Am I who I seem to be? Can I become what I would like to become? What would I like to be, to become?

This question remained with me for years. It's still with me today.

Twenty years have passed since that night in Pallet. What have I become? A canon. At least. It's less than nothing. It's my fault: I gave in, instead of doing without any security. Conformity with a bad conscience. But didn't my proud father also make concessions? Didn't he with his own hands hurl his book about the Trinity into the fire when the church ordered him to do so? Didn't he let himself be forced to say the Credo, to read from a piece of paper, to read it like a student, although he cried angry tears? Of course I hate the powers that humiliated him and are destroying me. And yet I'm in their service and accept their money and their privileges. The only one who never really gave in was and is my mother, Heloise. She did enter the convent, but only out of excessive love for Abelard. She never feigned submission, never renounced her love, never lied about her sexual desires, never pretended to have taken the veil out of love for God. She never said that you acted according to the will of God. For what is that, the will of God? Was it the will of God that I was fathered? Wasn't it blind fate, which one cannot escape? I was born without my will. I was abandoned without my will. I grew up here without my will. That I rode to Paris to study: was that my free will? What is it in people that drives them to do things that they don't want to do at all? What kinds of law control this world? I'll talk about that with Abelard. With whom else? Everyone else would answer with pious sayings, "It is God's mysterious will that guides you." If that is true, then what am I? A puppeteer's puppet. Or a trained animal. Where does that leave sin? Without free will, there is no sin. "God means well by you; he leads you with a loving hand." I laugh. The loving hand led Abelard and Heloise into bed, and then it led the young woman into the convent prison and Abelard to castration, and it didn't concern itself with me at all, the loving hand. My suspicion is it doesn't exist, this hand, there is no God, there are only coincidences. Didn't this God let his son play right into the hands of the heathen Jews? Did he watch as this son died on the gallows? Why? Does he see out of the farthest corner of his eye how three people, allegedly his children, suffer? And even if two of them were guilty, why does the innocent one suffer with them? What dark, secret connections rule in the plan of the world, if there is one?

I couldn't bear to be in my bed any more, in my room; I ran out of the house, I ran and ran, my horse in the stable whinnied after me, the dogs followed me, ran in front of me, blocked my path; they took it for a game at an unusual hour of the night. Had Abelard perhaps also roamed around like this once, sick and pursued by all the ghosts? He survived the illness and the crisis.

Abelard, Abelard. I was drawn to Paris. To him. When I returned to the house hours later, wet with dew and dead tired, Denise was standing in the doorway. She didn't ask anything. She said, I've made you a tea of linden blossoms.

Nothing more. That did me good. No question, no warning, nothing but this offer, this silent sign of love. Mother Denise.

Dawn was breaking. We remained sitting a little while longer. There were open questions, open wounds.

Denise, why didn't my mother take me with her to Paris?

That would have put her and you in danger. Mortal danger. Fulbert was frothing with rage. He swore revenge on the seducer, the seduced, and the child. They wanted to know that at least you would be saved. Do you understand?

I understand, oh yes, I understand.

Oh, my little one, don't torment yourself so, and me too. You had such a beautiful childhood, you were happy, you were loved, you also had an excellent private tutor. . . .

Yes, he was forbidden to teach in Paris, I know. He was the person who first taught me how to think. Abelard's thoughts were already in the air, even here, far away from Paris. Well, now, Denise, I won't torment you any longer. For me you are the best mother I could have. I'm eternally grateful to you. I would give my eyeteeth if I could stay here.

And I! What wouldn't I give to see you happy. But don't you think there is also someone in Paris who needs you?

Abelard? Oh, he. He needs nobody and nothing. He is his own God, his own church, his own universe together with its own heaven and its own hell. Who am I? A shadow that sometimes crosses his face and disturbs him.

What would you like to be to him?

What I am: his son. No: Heloise's present to him.

Denise didn't need to answer me; what could she have said? As luck would have it, so to speak, someone was coming toward the house. A farmhand. At least someone in a farmhand's clothes.

Who's that? He looks familiar to me.

Be quiet. Don't speak to him. He isn't right in the head. It could be dangerous if he recognizes you. But he probably won't recognize you.

The man came in, put a dead, still bleeding chicken on the table, looked at me, shook his head, and shuffled out again.

Denise, that's my former tutor! What's wrong with him?

They drove him crazy.

They? Who?

Well, now. He was forbidden to teach at the university, so he taught secretly, as he did at our place. They got on his trail and locked him up in the Saint-Médard monastery, where the insane are and the unpopular. Abelard got him out and brought him here. Since then he has lived here as a farmhand. Hidden.

Damned clergy.

They once locked your father up there too, for a short time, but he had not only enemies but also powerful friends, who freed him. Our poor Don Richard has no friends except Abelard.

And me!

I ran after him. I called his name. He stood still, but it was evident he didn't recognize me. He bowed, made the sign of the cross, and murmured, Credo, credo, credo, cre cre cre do do do. Then he made the sign of the cross again and went on. Then he met a farmhand before whom he stood still, bowed, made the sign of the cross, and murmured his Credo cre cre. There was no point in trying to talk with him. He had built himself a protective wall out

[126]

of these words that they had forced him to recite. I don't think he was crazy. His eyes were too clear. But he had decided once and for all to say nothing more.

Denise said he was the most hard-working farmhand on the property, except that every few months he would wring a chicken's neck.

What else does he do?

He locks himself in the tower room.

I crept up there in the evening. The door wasn't locked. No one ever dared to enter. I dared to. He acted as if he didn't notice me. He was sitting at the table, writing. But what was he writing there? What language was that? Not Latin, not Greek, not Hebrew, a completely foreign language. Perhaps one he had made up. No person should be able to decipher it. I am certain they were theological treatises and definitely to be taken seriously. But his retreat was to be absolute. No one was to know what he thought.

Would this also be my father's end: the final retreat into silence? No. Unthinkable. The lion will fight to his last breath.

And yet, he too had to lower his weapon more than once. The Credo of my poor private tutor and Abelard's Credo at the Synod of Soissons . . . And how many other thinkers has this church broken, condemned to silence, has burned them and their works at the stake. I was suddenly afraid for Abelard.

I had to go back to Paris. I, the foolish boy, I, the mediocre little student, what could I do for Abelard, for my father? It wouldn't help him if I were to wring a chicken's neck. But what should I do?

In any case I had to go back to Paris. Denise didn't hold me back. She got a bag ready with provisions for me and another with bread and salt; it was for Abelard.

I didn't wait for my foster father to return. There was nothing to talk about with him. It was good and lovely to see Denise again. I had experienced her warmth and love. So I rode away again. My heart was broken. The dogs didn't believe I was going; they accompanied me a long way, until they saw that I had crossed the boundaries of their territory. A shepherd's whistle called them back. But Paris called me.

The first thing I wanted to do was visit my friend Roger, although I couldn't expect to find him. He wanted to go on a trip and wouldn't be back yet. His landlady said, It's a good thing that you have come. They are all beside themselves.

Who? And why?

The students. Professor Abelard's students.

What's wrong with him?

He is ill.

Seriously ill?

So they say. They're carrying on as if he were on his death bed.

I ran as if my life depended on it, and perhaps it really did. His life and my life. Two students stood before his house like a police guard: no one was allowed in.

They recognized me and let me pass. I raced up the stairs. Again two watchmen. One of them was Roger.

What's wrong with him? Is it serious?

A nervous fever. He's delirious. He's talking with Bernard of Clairvaux, arguing with him. It has to do with Bernard's rejection of logic and dialectics. But most of it is incomprehensible. Listen, now he's singing.

Do quietem fidibus
Vellem ut te planctibus
Sic possem et fletibus
Lesis pulsu manibus
Raucis planctu vocibus
Deficit et spiritus.[3]

One of the songs that he wrote for Heloise's convent. A verse from the great Jephthah work. His voice sounded weak, but very clear.

3. I give rest to my strings / That I may communicate with you through / Lamentations and the shedding of tears. / With hands injured by strumming / And voice hoarse from wailing: / My spirit now fails. *Trans.*

Is he in his right mind?

Maybe, and maybe not. He often sings, but seems to be sleeping or only half conscious when he is doing so. If we ask him something, he doesn't answer.

How did it get this bad?

We don't know exactly. People say Bernard visited the Paraclete. That's when it began.

But Bernard was his friend.

Now he's his enemy. Go on in. But keep very quiet.

He lay there on his back, his hands folded across his chest, his eyes shut. A dead person lies like that.

I fell to my knees beside his bed and laid my head on the hard edge of the bed. A miserable bed. A rough blanket, horse blanket.

I sensed a movement, a hand felt its way over to me. I laid my face on this hand.

Now he spoke, Go out, Roger, don't let anyone in.

Without opening his eyes, he said, Have you come at last?

My heart was pounding as if it would burst. Father!

He squeezed my hand; he held it firmly.

Then he looked for something under his pillow. A crumpled piece of paper. He pressed it into my hand. Take it to the Paraclete; give it to Heloise.

But they don't allow me to go to her, and she doesn't want to see me.

Tell them at the gate that it is a letter from Abelard to Heloise. Seal the paper. Perhaps it's better that you don't see each other. Our Heloise suffers too much.

"Our Heloise," he said. How had I ever been able to hate the man who was my father.

Father, I said. I think I said it many times.

Go now, I'm tired, but I'm getting better. And for the time being we'll continue to be teacher and pupil. Fear the envy of those who seem to be your friends and fear the hate of my enemies. But you and I, we both . . .

Nothing more. I went. I went silently past Roger and the other guards, who stared at me but didn't speak to me. I held my hand pressed to the jacket pocket that contained Abelard's message to Heloise. A letter from my father to my mother. Whatever it said, the fact that I delivered it was the legitimation of my origin. Abelard to Heloise. My father to my mother. I should seal the letter, my father had said. I didn't own a seal. Whom could I trust? The physician. That was the most natural choice; the physician knew the secret. And he could tell me something about Abelard's condition.

Nothing serious. A little breakdown. Not the first. The earliest was in 1108. At that time he went home to Pallet to recover.

This time I was in Pallet!

To recover?

No and yes. I sought peace.

Did you find it?

How could I find it when a feeling was driving me back to Paris.

Did someone send you a message?

No. Why would they? I felt that I was needed in Paris. Or maybe not needed. I only felt that something was calling me and driving me. Tell me honestly: does it look bad for Abelard?

Not physically. He will recover quickly. But he feels ill on account of Bernard's hostility. Bernard simply doesn't want to understand him. Both are great men. What divides them is something that to me, a half heathen, appears to be a trifle, but for the two of them means a life and death battle. It's the matter of freedom of will. Abelard attributes to man a great spiritual freedom, which amounts to freedom of will. Bernard says that's a heresy.

Yes, the Pelagius story. An age-old story. Posse in natura, velle in arbitrio.[4] I know. They were struggling once again with the doctrine of original sin. Abelard spoke about it in a lecture on St. Augustine.

But now the quarrels are beginning again. I'm no theologian, only a physician, but when I deliver a baby, I can't believe that it was born full of malice. Just look at the eyes of a newborn: there is heaven in them. But you haven't come to talk about theology. What do you want of me?

4. The ability to do something lies in a person's nature, the will to do it lies in his judgement. *Trans.*

Nothing more than a seal on this letter.

A letter? That's a crumpled piece of paper with spots of mildew. Perhaps they are the traces of tears. Or drops of sweat. Hand it over. From whom to whom?

From Abelard to Heloise.

From your father to your mother, that is. Do you know what he is writing to her?

No. How could I abuse his trust.

So you weren't forbidden to read it?

No.

Perhaps he rather wished that you would read it? Wouldn't he otherwise have sealed the letter himself?

He didn't have a seal.

Nonsense. It's a great sign of trust from father to son. He wouldn't have given the letter to anyone but you.

But he couldn't know that I would come.

He counted on it that you would hear his silent wish. By the way, he mentioned your name several times in his fever.

I smoothed the crumpled letter.

"Lovingly concerned, dearest Sister . . ."

I threw the letter to the floor. Sister! What a lie. Sister. Beloved, bride, wife, anything but sister. And Heloise is supposed to accept this form of address? Won't she tear up the letter before she has read further? Sister. How friendly, how innocent, as if there had been nothing there at all. No burning passion. No well-known affair. Only brotherly and sisterly friendship and spiritual kinship.

But I was curious as to what Heloise was expected to read.

The letter began, as it were, in the middle of a passage; it was obviously the continuation of a letter that had preceded it.

And now the one point still remains to be discussed. It's the old complaint that you raise again and again. You have the nerve to take God to task about the way we were converted, instead of offering him the praise that is due to him for our conversion.

One can't be blind to this guiding grace of our God, and so I had very firmly believed that your bitterness would have dissolved into thin air before the obvious guiding grace. This bitterness is a great danger for you; it wears down your body and soul, it is your unhappiness and my anguish! You do promise very clearly and distinctly that you want to live to please me in everything; then fulfill your promise, don't torment me with it anymore, rather give me the one great joy and cast off this bitterness! If you remain attached to it as you have until now, then you can no longer please me and also cannot ascend to eternal salvation together with me. You promised to follow me into eternal damnation, and here you want to bring yourself to let me go alone to salvation? Do try, at least in this matter, to submit meekly to God's will! Otherwise you separate yourself from me, if I really am hastening to God – at least you think I am! This submission cannot be so difficult for you; it will open up the salvation of heaven to you and will let our union become a union of joyous thanks. Would it be easier for you to bear and would it upset you less if I had deserved my misfortune? Truly, then my tragedy would be a disgrace for me and a triumph for my enemies! Then their deed would be justified and would deserve full recognition; then the guilt would be mine, the contempt of the world would be mine; then no one would want to rail against what happened and pity me.

But why does he feel his tragedy is undeserved? Undeserved? The castration undeserved? Does he bring his theological thesis in here that guilt is only what happened with bad intent? Undeserved? Didn't he seduce an innocent girl and get her pregnant and then abandon and cast off the child? Undeserved? Undeserved? I put the letter away.

The physician said, Do read on.

I read on reluctantly:

Live well in the Lord, you handmaiden of the Lord. Once dear and precious to me in the world, now above all dear and precious to me in Christ. Farewell, once wife in the flesh, now sister in spirit and comrade-in-arms in the army dedicated to Christ.

Well, now, that sounded better, although Heloise would have preferred to hear other forms of address. Such as hers to Abelard: "Only beloved," "Dearest," "To my lord, no, to my father, to my husband, to my brother from his handmaiden, no, his daughter, his wife, no, his sister, to my Abelard from his Heloise."

Abelard, however, only addresses her as "sister."

The physician saw it differently. You don't have a sister, he said, that's why you don't know what the word can mean. Be quiet, listen: I had a sister, a twin sister, a twin soul; we loved each other very much, she was everything to me, we had the same character, we thought the same thoughts; neither she nor I married, because there was no one else we got along with as well. When we were eighteen, we both got sick, a form of the plague. I survived it, my sister died. Since then I've been alone. Do you understand?

Yes, but your sister was really your sister. Heloise . . .

It isn't the body that loves, but consciousness, do you understand? One can find a sister with whom one is more strongly connected than would be possible through physical love. Abelard loved Heloise more strongly when she was no longer his wife and lover. So, and now ride to the Paraclete and deliver the sealed letter and don't expect to speak to Heloise.

I expect to. I insist on it. She, who never lies, can't lie me out of existence.

The closer I came to the Paraclete, the stronger was my desire to see my mother or to speak to her, but my fear was also stronger: what did we have to say to each other?

Nothing. If not everything. But this wasn't the moment for that. I was only a messenger. Abelard had assigned me this role.

I had put the crumpled, sealed page in a clean vellum and tied it up. No strange eyes should see the true state of the letter and of its author.

My horse was confused. Now I hurried it, then I forced it to walk, and suddenly I urged it on again. Three times I circled around the convent wall. From a distance I heard the nuns singing. Certainly one of the hymns that Abelard had written the words for and composed for the convent. One of the voices, the solo voice, the precentor, that must be the prioress. Heloise.

Now you are singing and don't suspect that I'm bringing you the news from Abelard, who is seriously ill. Will she receive the letter right away and read it?

[133]

I knocked at the gate. A head appeared. A young voice. A postulant.

Here, give the letter to the prioress; it comes from Abelard, it's urgent.

Should you wait for an answer?

On my own initiative I said, Yes. Hurry. Abelard is ill. Very ill.

What an effect that had! The girl ran. I heard her steps on the cobbles. I thought, Now she's handing over the letter. Now Heloise is holding it in her hands. Now the singing has to break off. No, it didn't break off. Finally silence.

Now she'll go into her cell and read. Her hands will tremble. When she opens the clean vellum and removes the seal, will she be surprised at the condition of the letter that shows itself to her as it lay under Abelard's pillow, who knows how long, crumpled, sweat stained, smudgy? Will she answer? Will she guess the identity of the messenger? The little nun hadn't asked for my name. "Someone delivered the letter." Someone. A man.

Heloise reads; she searches for words of love between the lines. She finds exhortations. She finds an allusion to his condition: "If I really am hastening to God . . ." What must she think? What can she answer?

I won't know. She won't hand over a letter to an unknown person. After all, she doesn't know, my God, she doesn't know who the messenger is.

Should I wait? And if she doesn't give me a letter to take with me? Should I sit here like a dog who has been ordered: Sit?

I feel anger. I'm no dog that obeys the command of its master. Go, run, fetch . . .

But if Abelard is waiting for an answer?

Could I suspect what she was writing to him in this hour? Later on I would read it. Words of despair.

If I lose you, then I have nothing more to hope. Why should I then continue my pilgrimage here? I have only one consolation in this world: you! God, how cruel you are. All the force of fate, all its arrows were used up on me. And if fate ever finds yet another arrow: it won't find a spot on me that is still without a wound. . . .

I sat and waited. The day couldn't have been more beautiful: a summer day, not hot, full of the smell of hay and bitter herbs, the larks high above the fields, cuckoos calling still, the last, soon they will fall silent, when the grain is cut and bound into sheaves.

To sit like this. To stay like this. In peace. Why torment oneself? What's the use of all the talking and bickering? Abelard, Father, give up trying to convince your enemies of the truth! Come, take Heloise out of this convent; come, let's go to Pallet, there is peace there. Apple trees, sheep, Denise's quiet piousness. God's spirit over the good earth. To serve the unknown God with simple, humble work. Abelard, give up your diabolical arrogance. You don't know more than everyone else, namely, you know nothing. Come, learn the love of life! Save your beloved, your wife, your son, these prisoners of your fate. Do have pity. Are you capable of love? How would that be: a normal family in the country. But would I love my parents if they were simple people? Do I love, with all my stubbornness, only that legend that has been spun around the two of them? Am I perhaps the spiritual heir of my father: do I love ideas instead of realities? Isn't my life already wasted before it has really begun? I, a man gone astray. I, an eternally waiting dog. The loyal little dog of great masters. A foundling dog. I felt the urge to bark and to howl. Having to wait made me crazy. Was this humming of bees in my head or was it in the trees? Merciful bee choirs: they lulled me to sleep.

My horse woke me up; it whinnied because someone had approached. A nun, but without a letter, only with a pitcher of water and a piece of bread. Wait a little longer, she said and disappeared.

At least those inside were aware that someone was waiting and waiting. I gave the bread to my horse and poured the water into a stone bowl. The horse drank.

Something fell from above into the grass beside me. A small parcel. To Abelard. In Greek. I read, "To her only beloved after Christ from his only beloved in Christ."

I didn't see the hand that had written this and thrown it to me. Was she sure that the messenger didn't know Greek? Or was she sure that he did know it? Was he supposed to understand it? Did she know who the messenger was? I untied my horse; it whinnied loudly – Heloise had to hear it – then I galloped away, suddenly seized by the fear that messenger and message would come

[135]

too late and I would only be able to place the letter in a dead man's hands. I hurried my horse. When I got caught in a flock of sheep in a narrow pass I cursed with anger, but the curses were indistinguishable from prayers, Let him live, damn it, let me arrive on time, oh, you damned sheep, damned shepherd . . .

Finally Paris. Finally Abelard's quarters. Roger. Another loyal dog.

Is he alive?

Yes, and he's feeling better, but the fever is still too high. And now and then he asks: Not back yet? Now go to him, right away, I'll look after your horse, I'll rub it dry; you must have ridden like the devil, one of these days you'll break your neck, you fool.

I flew up the stairs, I stumbled over the threshold.

A sigh came from the direction of the bed. And then, very quietly, At last! Outstretched arms.

Did he mean me or the letter?

Ineradicable mistrust: he means Heloise, he means her letter. But the miracle occurred: he meant me too, he didn't tear the letter out of my hand, he put his arm around me. Around me. And then, very quietly, My son.

I couldn't hope for more on this earth. It was the height of happiness. "My son." Father. I had a father. And what a father!

A long embrace. I wasn't ashamed of the tears, neither mine nor his.

To die with him, now, at this moment . . .

It wasn't granted us.

Four weeks later Abelard stood behind the lectern again, thin and pale, but full of tension and fire. And I, I was one of his students again. We guarded our secret. But when our eyes met, we allowed ourselves a smile.

Hadn't I wanted to persuade Abelard to give up his scholarly life and to lead the normal life of the landed gentry? But the normal life – there was no such thing for Abelard. A show horse is no plow horse. The normal life – that was for people like me.

But was it really so normal? Is it a normal fate to be laid on the stone altar, a lamb bound hand and foot, and to be neither sacrificed nor saved? There it lies, the lamb, unable to free itself. It isn't even permitted to cry out, because the scream for help would not have been allowed to be heard, it would have destroyed Abelard's career. The lamb was silent.

Whoever thanked it for that?

Couldn't I have jumped up in a lecture and shouted, The one over there, the famous one, the great teacher, he is a rogue, a liar; he is married and has a son, me, look at me, and he denies everything, driven by his ambition, by his daemon, by Lucifer himself. Knowledge, knowledge, knowledge. But without love. A life that is a lie. He locked up his wife in the convent, forced her to become a nun. That's how it is.

And what would have ensued? Would Abelard have said, He is right?

The students would have shouted, Throw out this fool who is slandering Abelard.

Or, What's that to us? He's the greatest of our teachers, he is our future; it ill becomes us to judge him. We're here to learn from him, to let ourselves be carried along by the wind of the spirit. Abelard is the future.

I kept quiet. Of course I kept quiet. For whom was I important? Whom would my words have hurt? No one but myself. It would have been patricide. And with my father, my mother would have died too. And with the two of them I myself.

I kept quiet for another full year. But Abelard, with all advisable caution, did show me his trust from time to time. Now and then he invited me to accompany him on walks. Sometimes he took several other students along to serve as camouflage; then our discussions were nothing more than a continuation of the lecture.

Once we discussed the question whether it is a sin to carry out somebody's order when this order aims to do evil. And the other question: if someone forces someone else to do something bad together with him, is the consent of this other person then a sin? Abelard's old topic. He didn't take part in the conversation, and naturally I kept quiet too. Only he and I knew what was in question. Poor Abelard; two decades later he was still tormenting himself with the question of guilt. Much worse and yet much more honestly than St. Augustine. I have the suspicion that St. Augustine, while remorsefully confessing, derived a manifold pleasure from doing so: the pleasure of remembering his youth and the wild sins of his youth, the pleasure of public confession, the pleasure of proud self-humiliation, the pleasure of speaking with his God, and the pleasure of literary articulation. This above all, because he was a man of language. An orator and a poet. How he enumerates all the attractions and enjoyments that he had fully experienced and then fully overcome: the delight in choice foods, in beautiful music and melodious language, in women, in every kind of beauty! Remorse is cheap when one has had the pleasure. It's much bitterer to have nothing that one can regret.

And Heloise? She regretted nothing. Absolutely nothing. She suffered because she no longer had what she actually should have regretted. How Abelard, who had become an ascetic, tried to bring her to a penitent frame of mind! She wasn't even able to repent for his sake. Not for anything in the world, not even for the love of Abelard, and certainly not for the love of the suffering Christ (as Abelard so urgently asked her to do) did she want to make undone what really was a sin. Not repentance but quarreling with God, who robbed her of her beloved and thereby of her youth and life. Nothing but rebellion. Until Abelard firmly forbade her to complain any more. Then she was silent. Then she became, out of proud obedience, the prioress who requested advice from the experienced master Abelard. The request was seriously meant, of course, and yet it was the pretext for staying in constant and close contact with him. If it was no longer possible to live a common, natural marriage, then it was still possible to have this spiritual marriage. Heloise's nuns: her and Abelard's daughters. And I?

That year in which Abelard first really legitimized me, so to speak, he began to include me in this unusual form of family life. On our walks then we discussed much of what I later read in that great letter to Heloise about her convent. Strange that he asked me for my opinion about this and that rule, even though I had no experience with monastic life.

It seems to me today that Heloise knew exactly how she should and could run her convent and that she only wanted to hear from Abelard that he was in agreement with the changes that she wanted to make in the old Benedictine monastic rule. She was concerned that the clothing that Benedict ordered the strong monks to wear was too heavy and too rough for women. She was also concerned about eating and drinking and fasting, and whether nuns were allowed to invite other people, men or women, to a meal; she was concerned about the planning of the day: the laud at daybreak, then another short rest period in the dormitory, then the morning wash, then reading or singing in the cloister, then the prime, then the chapter with the reading from the book of martyrs and the meditation on it, and finally the abbess will speak and give orders or deal out reprimands and punishments. In the chapter every sister is allowed to voice her opinion, but the decision remains with the abbess, and she must be unconditionally obeyed.

At this point Abelard and I got into an argument.

And if what the abbess says is wrong and if her commands are senseless and needless? Even then?

Yes, even then.

And if all the other sisters are opposed?

Even then.

Abelard, that goes against your principles. Even you mutiny against your superiors' incorrect decisions, even you don't obey when an order seems stupid to you.

I obey when the order serves the spirit and the salvation of the soul. But I oppose pernicious ideology.

What do you mean by that?

In the Gospel the Lord says, I am the truth. He does not say, I am custom.

Abelard quoted from memory Pope Gregory VII, who in turn quotes Cyprian, the great authority: "Every habit, no matter how old or widespread it is, must recede before the truth in every case; a custom that stands in contradiction to the truth must be abolished."

Yes, but how does one know what the real truth is? Are you always certain that you know it? Isn't it sinful arrogance to think one has the truth and the others are mistaken?

An astonished glance: I am sure of myself when my thinking has eliminated all arguments that conceal the truth.

I must have had the devil in me when I asked, And the Holy Ghost? Do you put your thinking in the place of the Holy Ghost?

[139]

With the same right that the others put their antiquated ways of thinking in the place of the Holy Ghost.

How should I, for example, know whom I can believe?

No one other than yourself. There is a way of thinking that is purely logical, and there is a way of thinking that is in harmony with the innate knowledge of the divine truth.

Yes, but how can one differentiate between them?

True knowledge is living light, but knowledge that is only superficially acquired is cold and dead and doesn't place one under any obligation, least of all the obligation to love.

Father, you are unbeatable.

He laughed. Just try to argue with me; that is good for both of us.

We went back to the monastic rules for Heloise. In the convent the day was strictly regulated. There was hardly a moment in which a sister could be by herself. Work, prayer, singing, work, mass, work. I asked myself when the abbess had time to write letters to Abelard. At night. In sleepless nights, when she feels those stirrings in her body about which she writes. At night, plagued by longing. Poor Heloise.

How is it with the men? I asked.

What do you mean?

Are priests allowed to visit nuns?

To visit?

Is the abbess allowed to receive a man if he is a priest?

For strong reasons, yes. But there are hardly any strong reasons.

Well, perhaps to help her keep her nuns in check.

If she can't do that herself, she has to be deposed.

Or if she herself needs advice and consolation?

Abelard stood still and looked at me sharply. Are you someone's messenger, sent to me to transmit an admonition?

No.

Then mind your own business.

That was clear and sharp.

Now I too was clear and sharp. Are you, Abelard, allowed to visit Heloise?

I am allowed in important cases to visit the prioress of the Convent of the Paraclete.

I had to laugh. Oh, Father, how astute you are. Now I understand why your colleagues fear to get into disputes with you. One way or another you are always right. You call that dialectics, don't you?

That hit him. He was silent. On the way back he didn't say another word. It gratified me that this time I had won against him.

One day, in a lecture, Abelard brought up the role of women in the life of Jesus. The topic actually did not fit in with the lecture series on free will. Presumably Abelard did not intend to stick to the topic on that day; it seemed as if he wanted to give a lecture on poetics. He began by quoting an eclogue by Virgil, the one about the prophecy of the sibyl of Cumae:

And a violent change of ages begins anew.
Now Virgo is turning away, Saturn is beginning to reign again,
And a new race will be sent from heavenly heights.

How he managed to get from the heathen figure of Virgo to the topic of the virgin seemed to me quite precipitous, as if he had used Virgil only as a pretext for talking about something that was of the utmost importance to him. He began with the Maccabean mother who watched while heathens killed her seven sons because they didn't want to renounce their Jewish God. Then he came with a leap to the resurrections of the dead by Elijah and Elisha in the Old Testament, saying that it was always the requests of women that gave the prophets the power to raise the dead. On the whole, women had always been particularly blessed by the Lord: Jesus spoke with the Samaritan woman at Jacob's well, Jesus was a friend of Mary and Martha and Mary Magdalene, who followed him to the foot of the cross. He quoted something Jesus said to the stubborn heathen that I hadn't heard before: "Whores are more likely to enter the kingdom of heaven than are you." Then he spoke of the role virginity played already among the heathen, quoting St. Augustine: "When the ancient Romans discovered vestal virgins who broke their vow of chastity, they were buried alive." And Emperor Justinian enacted a law that any man who touched the virgins dedicated to God should be punished by death. And Pelagius's famous letter to Mauritius's daughter: "Those who break the marriage of the heavenly bridegroom bring down a heavier punishment on themselves than those who break an earthly marriage."

And further along: "That is why recently the Roman Church quite rightly made the strict regulation that women aren't even to be allowed to do penance in church if they have shamefully desecrated their body, which is dedicated to God."

And so on, and in conclusion then the utterly strange story about the blessed Eugenia, who with the knowledge – indeed at the request – of Bishop Helenus wore men's clothing in order to be admitted, unrecognized, to the community of monks. She even became abbot.

We students burst into laughter, and one of us said rather loudly, What idiots the monks were that they didn't smell the woman.

Abelard left us to our wild laughter and our dirty jokes and went.

There was something crazy about this scene. But who, besides me, understood that Abelard had spoken of himself, of himself and Heloise, and that he had made a public confession, absurdly disguised, incomprehensible for the students who saw no other connection with Virgil's eclogue than that the word virgin occurred in it. On that day I attempted to accompany Abelard. He tolerated me silently. Rather, he not only tolerated me, but wished me near. I felt that he had something to say to me and finally he did say it, What do you understand by virginity? I said, Being untouched by a man.

He said almost angrily, You've already been my student now for three years and haven't learned to think. As if it depended on the deed. A woman can lose her virginity for this or that reason and still be innocent, namely, if her heart isn't defiled by the willingness to commit a sin, not only the sin of unchastity, but any sin. Do you understand now? And with that he left me standing there.

I hadn't understood, or perhaps I had understood all too well. Did he want to tell me that Heloise wasn't a virgin, not because she had slept with him, but because she unceasingly continued to have a burning desire for him?

[142]

I ran after him and held on to him firmly. You were talking about my mother, I said. You spoke ill of her, you who seduced her when she was a pure virgin. You threw the firebrand into her. You robbed her of the most precious thing that a girl has. You . . .

Be quiet, boy. The most precious thing that she has is not the virginity of her body but the power of her love. This power is the cleansing fire that takes every stain from her. I seduced her, certainly, but I made her what she is: the strong woman. She is stronger than I am. She deserves the crown.

So you say now. In the lecture one could hear something else. Is that what you call dialectics? I call it duplicity. I hate you for that serpentine intelligence of yours!

I ran away, I ran and ran. I heard him try to catch up with me, but soon give up. I turned around: he had sat down on a rock and held his hand pressed to his chest. I was alarmed. Was what I had previously wished on him so intensely going to happen now? Had I succeeded in committing patricide, finally? How serious was my desire to murder him?

I turned back. He was still sitting on the rock. The sun burned searingly on the shadeless street. Bad for Abelard's delicate health. I pulled his scapular over his head and sat down beside him. What should I do, what should I say? I couldn't think anymore. Nothing and no one came to our help. We suffered. Galley slaves, chained together forever. Who had condemned us? Who was the guilty one? Certainly not I. And Abelard? How was he guilty? And I, for what was I doing penance? For my existence? Or was I also doing penance for my parents' guilt? But what guilt was that? Is life always guilt at the same time? Is one really born heir to original sin? Can't one be other than guilty?

How then does one become "holy?" Impossible with this condition to sin. Even the thought of a sin is a sin. Says Abelard.

I sit beside him and look at him. I see only his profile. It is sharp. He has aged greatly. There are deep furrows beside his nose. And his mouth: bitterly resigned, tired.

No, I don't hate him. I feel nothing but an unnameable agony. *Ecce homo.* One is born, grows up, studies, climbs up, fights, and it's all nothing but suffering. Now Heloise should come, now, and put her arms around her beloved to protect him from his revulsion at the world and fear of the world. Heloise is far away. But I, I am here. I put my arm around Abelard's shoulder. Will he shake it off? Will he find my pathetic attempt to comfort him irksome and quite disproportionate to the magnitude of anguish in his life? He submits to it. He reaches for my hand, which is lying on his shoulder, and holds it firmly. I sense that he is clinging to it. Then he begins to talk.

He talks of his death. They won't be satisfied until they have killed the deer. Of a hundred arrows, one hits the mark. Bernard is a sharpshooter. Once he loved me. He is great, oh yes, but he is hard. He wants the second crusade to the Holy Land. Killing in the name of Jesus is supposed to be meritorious. That is his mistake. He became a monk, but remained a knight. He says so himself. He calls himself the Chimera of his century: half monk, half knight. But the killing of the heathen, that is a holy war for him. His concept of a united empire. His idea of the universal church. He loves it when people call him the uncrowned emperor. His ambition is as boundless as his piety. He knows only one fear: that my way of thinking has a future. Bernard will outlive me, not only because he is younger than I am, but also because he is physically more robust. But he is mentally ill. I know it. Even a lion has nerves and is afraid of ghosts. His ghost is called Abelard and dialectics. Abelard and thinking. When I'm dead, my thoughts will be more powerful than his, because time doesn't stand still, even when the conservatives want to stop the wheel. It's a pity that Bernard doesn't understand me. William of Saint-Thierry doesn't understand me either. Peter the Venerable, he understands me. Do you know that he was the first person to have the Muslims' Koran translated into Latin? A man of the world. He too has a future.

Abelard talked and talked. But not a word about Heloise, not a word about me or for me. I understood: what mattered for him was only his academic work. To say it more sharply: what mattered was he himself.

Poor Heloise, what was left over for you? And for the sake of this little bit you entered the convent. For the sake of this little bit you loved him to the point of madness. What strange creatures women are. They see every little mistake in the fabric of a dress their neighbor wears, but they don't see the faults in their beloved. Blessed blindness. But did Heloise really not see through Abelard's character?

She sees through him, oh yes, I read that in her later letters. She knew him, but she loved him. Not blindly, certainly not that, but helplessly driven by the daemon of Eros, no: by fate. Who talks of free will? I laugh. I forgot that Abelard is sitting beside me.

What are you laughing about?

About you. About all the contradictions in your character. About your mistakes. And about the fact that you were never really aware that you have a son, your own legitimate and also spiritual son. I am nothing and no one to you. But you can't help that. You are the way you are, and everything that you teach about free will is nonsense. Farewell, Abelard.

He took hold of my arm. Stay. Can't even you understand me?

Oh yes. And that's the very reason I want to go. I don't want to wither beside you. You are the tree whose roots drink the water all around it, so that nothing remains for me. Heloise is withering too.

Now he flared up, That's not true! She lives, she works, she leads her convent with strength and wisdom, she lives her life. . . .

No, she lives your life, Abelard. She lives on the little that you send her. On the leftover scraps of your actual life. Abelard, she is dying of thirst and hunger, because she isn't getting what she needs: your love.

What are you saying? I don't love her? What do you know about it? I love her with all my strength. My strength. And I love her in my way. In that way that is given and allowed me and seems beautiful to me. It is Heloise who doesn't understand how much more beautiful and also more appropriate this form of love is to her greatness and her rank. I want to tell you something: like all women she clings to an idea of love that wants to possess the beloved and be protected once and for all. But love wants change. Love is a spiritual path and not a comfortable house. I swear to you, my and Heloise's son: I love your mother as ever a man has loved, but I love her so that it is to the benefit of both of us.

Very nicely put. But a word struck me there that doesn't fit so smoothly into your speech.

And that is?

Heloise is a woman and clings like all women to her idea of love. Like all women. Didn't you say that? Like all women. Doesn't that in itself sound derogatory to you? I have often noticed that you praise women but think of them as the weak sex, with whom one must be lenient, because by nature they are more susceptible to evil. The old story of Eve, thought up by men. It is unworthy of you to think like that, especially when you are talking about Heloise. Is she weaker than you? Didn't you compose the song of praise to Jephthah's daughter? Do you think I don't know you're the poet? Who was stronger: Jephthah or his daughter?

Nevertheless, Heloise needed my protection when she was chased away from Argenteuil.

She needed it because men rule, and they rule against women.

The apostle Paul said clearly . . .

Yes, yes, I know: The man is the head, the woman is to obey him. The head: well, one thinks with the brain in the head. The man thinks for the woman. She doesn't need to think, she should only obey. However, I know a woman whose brain is capable of thought like a man's, and she has already proven that with philosophical works.

I was her teacher.

So she has nothing from herself, rather everything only from you.

I didn't say that.

But you're thinking it.

Why are you tormenting me?

Because I think. I too have learned how to think from you. Allow me to think further: Do you approve of Heloise being prioress?

How should I not approve of it? Though it does seem dangerous to me when women are provided with the same authority as men, that is, when they stand as abbesses at the head of convents just as men stand as abbots at the head of monasteries.

I don't understand; what difference does it make? If a woman is capable of running a convent like an abbot, why shouldn't she have the same rights?

Because it isn't in the nature of a woman to rule. She is more easily corrupted than a man. Therefore, in accordance with her nature, she cannot occupy a high position in the church, such as that of bishop.

Is bishop a high rank? Why can't a woman at least be a canon, as you are?

Here the word of the church and tradition is valid.

Abelard, you taught us to think. I am thinking now. Did Christ say: I am the tradition, or did he say: I am the truth?

There are traditions that are closer than others to the truth announced by Christ and embodied in him.

Yes, yes, Abelard, the unbeatable dialectician.

I am not concerned with being unbeatable. I am only concerned about the truth.

And you know the truth, because it is the result of your thinking, isn't it?

So it is.

But other people think too and arrive at other results. Are they then wrong?

What are you aiming at?

Something far away. For the moment not far away at all. I would only like to know if you really believe that you are stronger than Heloise because you are a man and succeeded in seducing a woman, getting her pregnant, and sending her into the convent.

Abelard stood up abruptly. It's not for you to judge us.

No? It isn't for me? Am I not your son? Isn't my fate linked with both of yours? Am I not suffering enough for your sake?

Had he even listened to me? He had turned to go. The invisible door had shut once again, and once again the old, bitter hatred came over me. Coward! I said, coward.

But it cut me to the quick to see him go away. Was he limping? I had never noticed it before, nor that he let his shoulders fall forward. Abelard had gotten old. How old? He was forty when he fathered me. I am twenty-two, so he is sixty-two. What caused him to get old so quickly? He was never very healthy, always susceptible to nervous fever. The excessive work. The many enemies. The mob of conservatives, led by Bernard of Clairvaux. Abelard hadn't said anything about it to me, but I knew from Arnold, his pupil and defender, that they were preparing a council in Sens, in which Abelard was supposed to be found guilty of heresy on account of his doctrine of the Trinity and his thesis on free will, to which he ascribed too much and crucial significance in comparison with the effect of grace. "Pelagianism" they called it. How feverishly they dig, said Arnold; how they twist every word of Abelard's until they find the sign of the devil. How they spy on him; how they smuggle their spies into his lecture room; how they incite some of his students to ask him incriminating questions. How they don't understand and don't want to understand that philosophy and theology also turn with the wheel of history and that new times need a new consciousness, so that the spiritual life will be advanced. The spirit must live, but it lives where it wants, and not where Abelard's enemies allowed or rather ordered it to live. From Arnold I found out that they wanted to send Abelard into exile, where he would once and for all be condemned to silence.

I followed Abelard with my eyes. He went slowly; he really did limp. I ran after him. I soon caught up with him. He didn't stop, he said nothing; I heard that his breathing was labored. So I trotted along beside him. Finally I couldn't stand it anymore.

Father, I said, forgive me.

He kept walking, and while walking he said, You think I didn't know my guilt?

If he had now said, "You too forgive me," then I am certain that every trace of hatred and bitterness in me would have been extinguished.

But he didn't say it. He kept walking. Then I left him and took off running without knowing where I was going. Let him do what he wanted. Let happen to him what he himself had brought about.

I ran and ran. It didn't help. What if he fell over now and died? I turned back, but didn't find him. He must have gone into a house. He had sought refuge somewhere. The help that I had refused him. Guilt weighed against guilt: now I was the guilty one.

I waited until evening before I dared to go to his apartment. He wasn't there, but he must have come back because his shoes were dusty; it was the dust of the streets we had walked on, one beside the other, for an eternity, so it seemed to me now. I ran to my friend Roger; he wasn't at home either. I ran to my friend the physician. He too was out. To whom could I go in my concern?

Where might Abelard be? Ill somewhere. And without Heloise. Without the comforting hand that would wipe the sweat of death from his brow. Should I ride to the Paraclete? But would Heloise come out from behind her walls? And where should she find him?

Perhaps he had fled to her.

Or was he already in the hand of his enemies?

I ran back to his apartment. But his possessions lay there untouched. Was that proof of his return? I sat down on the threshold. A dog who expects his master. I fell asleep.

His step woke me.

Thank God, I cried, there you are.

Where else should I be? Why are you worried about me?

Aren't you my father?

Yes, yes. Now you can go and get some sleep.

Father, you're ill!

Do you think so? And what if I am? Death is more welcome to me than any hour of life.

And your work?

I've done it. Now go and get some sleep.

I hesitated at the door. He called me back. Wait! Here, take this. Perhaps you'll understand some things better.

He handed me a sheet of paper. By the light of a street lamp, I read:

With hands injured by strumming
And voice hoarse from wailing:
My spirit now fails.

Then I heard his voice. For the first time, he called me by name, which he had always avoided.

[149]

Astrolabe! Come back up again.

Sit down.

He began to write. I sat in the darkness and watched Abelard as he wrote without lifting the pen from the paper, in a great sweep. Then he sealed what he had written. Take that, he said, and bring it to Heloise after I have been taken away and locked up.

Father, I cried, don't wait until they come to get you. Come, I have my horse, let's escape to Pallet.

Child, he said (I heard that word for the first time), child, I'm not going to flee. Fate takes its course. I've said what I must say. And when I am dead, go to the Paraclete. I shall be buried there.

Father, I cried – or screamed – you shouldn't die. You should save yourself for us, your students, for theology, for Heloise, for me, I beg of you!

What should remain, remains. In thousands of my students I've sown the seeds of the new. If three of them carry on my theology, I have not lived in vain. But now I am tired.

I left but remained sitting on the threshold of his house. A policeman drove me away. I came back again. So did he. He took me for a beggar or a drunk. Finally, toward midnight, Roger came. He had been looking for me. I told him why I was sitting there, keeping watch. He convinced me that there was no sense in waiting. People weren't going to lead Abelard away like a criminal. They would only forbid him to teach, yet again, and lock him up in a monastery, yet again, nothing new, but before that he would have to make a formal appearance before a council. He would know how to defend himself, thanks to his astuteness.

If he still wants to defend himself. He's tired, Roger, tired, and probably also ill.

You may be right, but there is no sense in sitting around here like a watchdog. Go home.

When I went to see Abelard the next morning, a canon who lived there told me that he had been picked up a short while ago by a carriage bearing the Cluny coat of arms.

So it was Cluny. That was no place for a banishment. The abbot of Cluny was Peter the Venerable. He was well inclined towards Abelard. Cluny, that meant he was saved.

I fetched my horse, I rode like a madman, I overtook the carriage in which Abelard was sitting; the mounted attendants wouldn't let me get close to it. I cried, Abelard, I'm with you! But he couldn't hear me or see me: there were curtains in front of the windows. I remained on the track of the carriage. So I saw that it really did pass through the gateway of Cluny.

Abelard was with Peter the Venerable. I asked to speak with the abbot. He came out, without hesitation. He didn't allow me to go to my father. He's very weak, he said, and any excitement could cost him his life. I'll keep you informed. Get rested, eat and drink, spend the night here, ride back, and wait. Your father is in the best of hands here. I'll also keep your mother informed. But you keep silent. If they ask you where Abelard is, you don't know, and that isn't a lie. I'll take him to a nice, quiet place where he can recover and work.

That place was the Saint-Marcel Priory. Abelard was well taken care of there.

One spring day, Abbot Peter sent a messenger telling me to come; Abelard wasn't well.

When I arrived, he had just died. The date was 21 April 1142.

In the European Women Writers series

Artemisia
By Anna Banti
Translated by Shirley D'Ardia
Caracciolo

Bitter Healing
German Women Writers, 1700–1830
An Anthology
Edited by Jeannine Blackwell and
Susanne Zantop

The Maravillas District
By Rosa Chacel
Translated by d. a. démers

Memoirs of Leticia Valle
By Rosa Chacel
Translated by Carol Maier

The Book of Promethea
By Hélène Cixous
Translated by Betsy Wing

*The Terrible but Unfinished Story of
Norodom Sihanouk, King of Cambodia*
By Hélène Cixous
Translated by Juliet Flower MacCannell,
Judith Pike, and Lollie Groth

The Governor's Daughter
By Paule Constant
Translated by Betsy Wing

Maria Zef
By Paola Drigo
Translated by Blossom Steinberg
Kirschenbaum

Woman to Woman
By Marguerite Duras and Xavière
Gauthier
Translated by Katharine A. Jensen

Hitchhiking
Twelve German Tales
By Gabriele Eckart
Translated by Wayne Kvam

The Tongue Snatchers
By Claudine Herrmann
Translated by Nancy Kline

The Panther Woman
Five Tales from the Cassette Recorder
By Sarah Kirsch
Translated by Marion Faber

Concert
By Else Lasker-Schüler
Translated by Jean M. Snook

Slander
By Linda Lê
Translated by Esther Allen

Daughters of Eve
*Women's Writing from the German
Democratic Republic*
Translated and edited by Nancy Lukens
and Dorothy Rosenberg

Celebration in the Northwest
By Ana María Matute
Translated by Phoebe Ann Porter

On Our Own Behalf
Women's Tales from Catalonia
Edited by Kathleen McNerney

[153]